THE WIDOW OF WEEPING PINES

NARRATIVE OF A MAD WOMAN

AMANDA MCKINNEY

HH TISEVICH

Paperback ISBN 979-8-9862527-1-1
eBook ISBN 979-8-9862527-0-4

Editor(s):
Nancy Brown, Redline Proofreading
Pam Berehulke
Donna Rich
Cover Design:
Damonza

Amanda
MCKINNEY
AUTHOR OF SEXY MURDER MYSTERIES

https://www.amandamckinneyauthor.com

DEDICATION

For Nancy, an unexpected light in my life. I can say with full
confidence that my books would be shit without you.

ALSO BY AMANDA MCKINNEY

NEW Thriller Series - NARRATIVE OF A MAD WOMAN:

The Widow of Weeping Pines

The Raven's Wife (Coming January 2023)

The Lie Between Her (Summer 2023

The Keeper's Closet (Summer 2023)

NEW Romantic Suspense Series - ON THE EDGE:

Buried Deception

Trail of Deception (2023)

Lethal Legacy

The Woods (A Berry Springs Novel)

The Lake (A Berry Springs Novel)

The Storm (A Berry Springs Novel)

The Fog (A Berry Springs Novel)

The Creek (A Berry Springs Novel)

The Shadow (A Berry Springs Novel)

The Cave (A Berry Springs Novel)

Devil's Gold (A Black Rose Mystery, Book 1)

Hatchet Hollow (A Black Rose Mystery, Book 2)

Tomb's Tale (A Black Rose Mystery Book 3)

Evil Eye (A Black Rose Mystery Book 4)

Sinister Secrets (A Black Rose Mystery Book 5)

BESTSELLING SERIES:

Cabin 1 (Steele Shadows Security)

Cabin 2 (Steele Shadows Security)

Cabin 3 (Steele Shadows Security)

Phoenix (Steele Shadows Rising)

Jagger (Steele Shadows Investigations)

Ryder (Steele Shadows Investigations)

Her Mercenary (Steele Shadows Mercenaries)

BESTSELLING SERIES:

Rattlesnake Road

Redemption Road

The Viper

And many more to come...

AWARDS AND RECOGNITION

JAGGER (STEELE SHADOWS INVESTIGATIONS)
2021 Daphne du Maurier Award for Excellence in Mystery/Suspense 2nd Place Winner

RATTLESNAKE ROAD
Named one of POPSUGAR's 12 Best Romance Books to Have a Spring Fling With
2022 Silver Falchion Finalist

REDEMPTION ROAD
2022 Silver Falchion Finalist

THE STORM
Winner of the 2018 Golden Leaf for Romantic Suspense
2018 Maggie Award for Excellence Finalist
2018 Silver Falchion Finalist
2018 Beverley Finalist
2018 Passionate Plume Honorable Mention Recipient

THE FOG

Winner of the 2019 Golden Quill for Romantic Suspense
Winner of the 2019 I Heart Indie Award for Romantic Suspense
2019 Maggie Award of Excellence Finalist
2019 Stiletto Award Finalist

CABIN 1 (STEELE SHADOWS SECURITY)
2020 National Readers Choice Award Finalist
2020 HOLT Medallion Finalist

THE CAVE
2020 Book Buyers Best Finalist
2020 Carla Crown Jewel Finalist

DIRTY BLONDE
2017 2nd Place Winner for It's a Mystery Contest

LET'S CONNECT!

Text **AMANDABOOKS to 66866** to sign up
for Amanda's Newsletter and get the latest
on new releases, promos, and freebies! (Don't worry, I have
no access to your phone number after you sign up.)
Or, you can sign up below.

Amanda
MCKINNEY
AUTHOR OF SEXY MURDER MYSTERIES

https://www.amandamckinneyauthor.com

WIDOW OF WEEPING PINES

Obsession turns deadly in this sleepy little coastal town.

Therapist and struggling author Betty Lou Abbott has a secret, one she keeps locked in the basement of the historic mansion she inherited from her late husband. Her fiancé, Ian, also has a secret: he is having an affair with one of Betty Lou's clients. She thinks so, anyway.

As Betty Lou's life becomes intertwined with the beautiful, successful Carmen Marquis, her intention to expose the affair turns into a dangerous obsession. Especially when she learns there is more to Carmen than meets the eye.

Caught in the middle of this cunning pair of women is Nicholas Stahl, a crooked detective who is determined to prove the truth—that one of them is a cold-blooded killer.

Two women—one crazy, one ill—and both have **secrets they would kill for.**

Two men—**one innocent, one ruthless.**

All four will leave you wondering who you can trust.

1

BETTS

*S*ometimes I wish my husband would die.

Do you ever feel like that?

Do you ever think how much better your life would be if your significant other would just keel over and die from a heart attack? Perhaps at the gym, or while raking leaves, or shoveling snow. Or maybe something a bit more cinematic, like an eighteen-wheeler taking him out on the way to work.

Quick, easy, done.

Just like that, the cancer in your life is eliminated.

Okay, fine, *cancer* is a bit dramatic, but that's how it feels sometimes. A constant battle of trying to be content, but then also feeling like you're trapped, your mind and body slowly being consumed by this *thing* that you don't want to become. All while knowing, deep in your soul, that you are no longer where you were meant to be. Knowing that every day that you don't act, you sink a little deeper into that black hole of hopelessness.

I just don't get marriage, a legally binding contract that demands you will:

A: Love someone unconditionally until death (and they, you).

B: Be a committed caregiver if the need arises (no matter the situation).

C: Never act upon feelings for another human being—ever. Not once. Not a single time.

D: Stand by your significant other's side, even if they can no longer pay the bills.

It is *absurd*.

The average lifespan is eighty years. Let's say you get married in your early thirties (or twenties, if you're Southern). This means for *sixty years* you have legally bound yourself to love and live with only one person—no matter how much they *or you* change.

Think about how much you changed from birth to age thirty. It is safe to assume you will change the same amount from age thirty to age sixty. Your thoughts, plans, desires, and priorities, they all change according to the life lessons we inevitably learn. Yet you're legally bound to *one* person.

I think about addicts in this scenario—blame it on the day job.

Example: you are addicted to booze, and the man you chose to marry is also an alcoholic. Birds of a feather. Ten years into your marriage, you decide to drop the habit. Your husband supports this decision (because what else is he going to say?).

However, as weeks turn into months, you two begin to drift apart. He is still drinking daily, while you are sober. Social events are suddenly odd and uncomfortable. Your home, once a sanctuary of sorts, is now a place of tension filled with words unsaid.

Your husband wishes you would drink with him, and this makes you feel guilty. So, you begin to resent him for not quitting alcohol, as you did. Naturally, he feels these vibes from you, and so he feels guilty for drinking in front of you.

It's a vicious, vicious cycle of unspoken guilt.

You are suddenly two people with very different priorities and perspectives on life. Yet, because you signed a document, you are legally required to stay in your marriage.

It makes absolutely no sense.

I know wishing harm on your husband is a bit uncomfortable to think about, but I am certain that every wife has felt this way at one time or another. *If he would just die, my life would be so much better.*

It is estimated that thirty percent of Americans struggle with depression. Think about that. Thirty *million* people are walking around depressed.

My theory? They're all just married.

Joke.

My theory is that they are not depressed. These people have simply lost touch with who they really are. Their internal light, that innate zest for life, has dimmed because they have slowly accepted whatever role society has boxed them into.

Wives trapped into being the same woman their husband married, even though someone else—someone very different and unacceptable to this husband—is *screaming* to get out. Thirty million people craving something more, something better. A different kind of life that makes them feel passion, that fire that makes us feel like we are really *living*.

It is an unceasing battle between courage and guilt. Guilt derived from your desire to break the vow of marriage battling with the spark of courage you feel after reading an inspirational post on social media. *Life isn't lived unless you seek true happiness.* Self-care, and all that bullshit.

So, which is it?

Am I supposed to honor my marriage, stay for the kids, whatever, or am I supposed to sever this legally binding commitment and seek true happiness—like Julia Roberts in that one movie?

Does it mean I'm weak if I leave my marriage? That I didn't try hard enough, wasn't strong enough, didn't practice mind-over-matter and "choose" happiness. Am I the definition of selfish for breaking up my family? *Or* would I be one of those women who people envy, look at, and say, "Good for her. She did it."

Which is right? Which is wrong?

Now you feel me, don't you? Now you understand where I'm coming from. Bottom line? Everyone wins if the husband would just keel over and die.

My name is Betty Lou Abbott. That's right—Betty Lou. As in bucktoothed, uneducated, Arkansan hillbilly Betty Lou. I go by Betts. Because *anything* is better than Betty Lou, right?

I have strawberry-blond hair, shoulder-length because it is so thin that if I grow it any longer, I am mistaken for Gollum's stunt double. Seriously, long hair for me equals a total of ten strands running down my back. Come to think of it, the *Lord of the Rings* character and I also share the unfortunate reality of having eyes too large for our faces.

I'm being dramatic. I'm not ugly, I'm not pretty. I'm just plain. Plain-Jane Betty Lou. They called me this in high school.

I am completely forgettable—or *was*, I should say, but we'll get into that later.

I am thirty-nine years old, a therapist turned writer.

Author-Doctor Abbott—always doctor, a title I squeeze into as many conversations as possible—and up-and-coming writer.

I've self-published two books, one a dystopian romance about a man and woman who find themselves trapped inside a dream, and the other, a horror with a Western flair. I write under the pseudonym Grey Sterling. Sounds smart, right? Better than Betty Lou—doesn't take much.

Anyway, I am working feverishly to finish the next book, a sci-fi/young-adult something. Not that anyone is knocking down my door to publish it. My last book peaked at number 147,479 in the online bookstore. I believe they call that a flop.

Before deciding to try my hand at writing, I worked as an underpaid middle school counselor. Dr. Betts, the students called me. It was the worst three years of my life. Scratch that—the second worst.

I am infertile. I think so, anyway. I've had three unexplained miscarriages. I've been poked, prodded, scanned, medicated. Nothing helps. That's all I care to say about that.

I am a widow and a newly-minted fiancée with zero intention to follow through with the nuptials (I'll explain this later).

My husband, Jack, died three years ago tomorrow. We had no kids—not from lack of trying—and so my consolation prize was a measly life insurance payout and a historically registered stone mansion tucked deep in the evergreens of his tragic hometown. A teeny-tiny dot in the Pacific Northwest called Weeping Pines, surrounded by miles of untamed wilderness.

This is where my story begins, and it is also where it ends.

It is going to be an uncomfortable ride, I can promise you that. But it is an honest, no-holds-barred story that you will relate to on a level you won't want to admit. You will love me, hate me, wish that it was me who would get run over by a logging truck.

Regardless of your perception, it is *my* story. One of restlessness, pain, triumph, and courage.

In a world filled with lazy assholes, I set out to change my circumstances. I could act, or do nothing at all.

I chose to act.

2

BETTS

$\mathcal{I}$t is autumn in Weeping Pines, a dizzying kaleidoscope of color. The trees are clothed in blazing reds, vibrant oranges, vivid yellows. I can only imagine what they would look like if the sun peeked out every now and then.

Weeping Pines lives under a massive cloud of bleakness. It is constantly gray. Every morning, a cloud descends upon the town like a virus sweeping through the woods. In the afternoons, the light wanes to nothing more than a dull illumination. A weird blue glow that makes my pale skin appear translucent and the veins pop like a road map.

I now understand why vampire movies are filmed in this region of the United States.

It is one of those predictable dreary afternoons. According to the weatherman, Weeping Pines is in the middle of a cold snap, with daily temperatures only reaching the mid-fifties. A sign of a bitter winter to come.

A gust of wind welcomes me as I step out of my BMW. Dead leaves spin around my boots as I slam the door, the sound echoing through the pines. A crow calls out angrily from his perch above me, displeased at my arrival, then swoops away and disappears into the woods.

I button my wool coat and tighten the black scarf I threw on at the last minute. After sliding my keys into my pocket, I step onto the narrow footpath worn by decades of mourners' dragging feet.

I weave my way through the weathered, crooked headstones, my vision laser locked on the edge of the cemetery.

Every year I visit this place, on this day, the anniversary of Jack's death.

Every year, a single black rose lies perfectly centered on the ground in front of my deceased husband's headstone.

A rose that I did not place there.

My pulse quickens as I close in on the corner of the cemetery.

There it is again. A beautiful, long black rose. Its flawless, butter-soft petals and vibrant green stem glare at me from the ground. Taunting me.

I pull up my hood, bow my head, and stare at the headstone under my lashes.

At the rose.

And as I do every year, I feel like I am being watched.

3

NICHOLAS

Olympic Mountains

There is always an eerie silence that surrounds a dead body.

Not just from the lack of life in the corpse itself, but also in the nature around it. There is a stillness, a quietness reserved only for moments like these.

I keep my flashlight low, slowly sweeping the beam along the forest floor while mentally cataloging anything that seems odd or out of place. A broken branch, overturned dirt, unnatural tracks. I notice the beginning of frost on the vegetation. Much too early. It's going to be a long winter.

I've never liked the winter. Bad things happen in the cold.

I tilt my head to the sky and blow out a long breath, watching the cloud of vapor roll on the wind and slowly fade away. Through the trees, I spot erratic pops of light from the first responders' flashlights.

As I emerge from the tree line, I frown at the lack of crime scene tape.

"Detective Stahl." A young, uniformed officer I don't recognize startles at my abrupt arrival and shines a flashlight in my face. "What are you doing here?"

I step around him, staring at the woman hanging from the tree at the far end of the clearing. Her bare feet are suspended at eye level of the three silhouettes standing below her.

A klieg light has been erected on the edge of the clearing, illuminating the woman's white nightgown in an almost supernatural glow. It is then I realize how truly dark the night is. If I hadn't known she was hanging from a rope, I might think she were floating.

The kid jogs after me. "Sir?"

He should be asking me to sign in.

I glance over my shoulder. "A detective should respond to every unattended death scene."

"But, sir, this is a reported suicide."

"Whether it be reported as suicide, homicide, accident, or natural."

"Oh. Yes, sir. Sorry, sir."

We set off down the footpath worn by the first responders before us, our flashlights guiding the way.

"What's your name, kid?"

"Jorge. Officer Enzo Jorge."

"That's right. Hired three months ago, yes?"

"Right."

"Never assume anything when you respond to a call, regardless of what dispatch told you." I gesture to the group standing below the dangling body. "Because this was reported as a suicide, the first responders didn't practice correct crime scene protocols, and therefore have walked all over the scene, potentially trampling valuable evidence—if it is, in fact, a crime scene."

Jorge nods enthusiastically, leaning toward me with an eagerness I recognize. I was like that twenty years ago.

"Anything and everything should be considered evidence," I say. "Whether physical or testimonial. And you need to catalog it all, and then tell me, the detective, *everything* once I arrive."

"Yes, sir."

We step over a rotting tree trunk. "Remember, people tend to take shortcuts when they hear the word suicide. Don't be that idiot, okay? The victims' families deserve better."

"Yes, sir."

Heads turn as I pick my way through the thick, gnarled brush.

Two officers and a sheriff's deputy linger below the corpse dangling in the wind. One is smoking a cigarette, one is holding a steaming cup of coffee, and the third looks the worse for wear. Likely it's his first time working the graveyard shift, and based on the green circle around his mouth, maybe even his first dead body.

I recognize the deputy as Dennis Wilburn. The veteran turned sheriff's deputy who is about ten years past his prime, in my opinion. He is tired, mentally and emotionally, this reflecting in the quality of his work.

Dennis turns to me, his cheek swollen with sunflower seeds—always BBQ. I've never seen the deputy without a pack on him, whether at five in the morning or eleven at night, like it is now.

"Stahl." Dennis breaks away from the uniformed officers. "Thought you were on a fishing trip."

"Got canceled." I swat at a bug zipping around my head, attracted to the light. "What have we got?"

"Suspected suicide. You can see scrape marks and

broken twigs on the trunk of the tree where she climbed up. Some kids out smoking dope saw it and called it in."

"Where are the kids now?"

"Called their parents and let 'em go. One vomited all over the place." He jerks his chin toward a patch of slimy grass. "Don't step over there."

I nod, contemplating the body, which is hanging from what appears to be a manila rope, about three quarters of an inch in diameter, if I had to guess. Typical rope found at any hardware store.

Her neck is obviously broken, bent backward at a ninety-degree angle. Long gray hair hangs in strings down her back, a knotted strand stuck in her mouth. Her skinny, pale arms are scratched, her ankles too, but with streaks of blood. She's wearing no shoes, only a white nightgown.

Her body catches the wind, slowly twirling in the breeze, the rope creaking loudly under her weight.

"God, it's creepy, isn't it?" Dennis mutters.

I disagree, but learned long ago to keep my innermost thoughts to myself. "How long you think she's been dead?"

"Few hours." He spits a kernel on the ground. "No identity on her yet, and there are no missing persons matching her description, so who knows? Probably some druggie."

Her name is Edith Clarke.

"She's got a tattoo on her ankle." He nods to her foot. "Best I can tell, a snake."

Not a snake. It's the letter S, a tribute to her third husband . . . or was it her fourth?

Dennis sniffs. "I'll call around to the tattoo shops in the morning, see what I can find. I've got Marge coming with the ladder. Once we cut her down, we'll take her to Eddie's, have him check her prints."

Eddie is the county medical examiner. "Eddie's" is the nickname for the morgue.

"I'll also have him run a toxicology on her. Probably high on meth or somethin', got in a fight with her boyfriend, lost her mind, hung herself. Not the first one."

The toxicology test will show that Edith wasn't on drugs, but that she was drunk. Likely on her favorite gin, Tanqueray.

The deputy turns to me, tilting his head to the side. "You came all the way out here. See anything that should make me record this as anything other than a suicide?"

"Nope."

Nothing other than the piece of vegetation in her hair that suggests she spent time on her back, possibly being strangled in the grass before someone tied her up and staged the scene. I'd bet my ass if the deputy spent more than five minutes searching the ground, they'd find not one but two sets of human tracks.

"Well . . ." I glance at my watch. "Looks like you've got everything covered here."

The deputy nods. "Go home. Get some sleep."

I won't sleep, but I will go home. I'll pour myself a big glass of whiskey, or maybe even open that old bottle of champagne from the fridge.

Because the thing is, Edith was a bitch.

She deserved it.

4

BETTS

I stumble through the woods of my backyard, my oversized UGGs crunching on a blanket of pine needles and dead leaves. My body feels disconnected from my head, like a malleable twig saturated from too much rain. I love this feeling, the rare moment when my shoulders aren't up to my ears and my jaw isn't clenched like a wooden doll's.

I have the perfect buzz. That heady, floaty sensation where you just can't help but smile.

Thank God for vodka.

The clouds have parted, just barely, allowing slices of late-afternoon sun to cut through the trees like swords of fire. I grin at the light, reveling in the rare thrill. The leaves seem to sparkle with pride, unaccustomed to sunlight in this dark, dreary town.

It is the first day that I notice the smell in the air. That fresh, crisp scent of fallen leaves. Autumn has become my favorite season in Weeping Pines. A season of maturing, ripening. Of death to self, followed by new birth. A season of drinking a pint of vodka on a weathered picnic table in the woods behind your home—before noon.

I check my watch, squinting at the blurred Roman numerals.

I am late. (I think.)

I stumble again, my boots slipping in a patch of mud. It is a slow-motion stumble, a side effect of the alcohol-induced delay between my brain and body. I right myself and press on.

Coffee. Must get coffee.

I stumble twice more before finally making it back to my home, a large stone house registered with the state historic preservation office. It is my little medieval castle, guarded by thick, mature trees. Despite the ghoulish vibe, the home is beautiful, encased in leafy vines that crawl up the sides, all the way to the roof. Today, as is the case with every October, the vines have turned from green to bright shades of red and orange, like spatters of paint against a gray canvas.

The Gadleigh Estate is notorious in Weeping Pines, its thick stone walls guarding secrets of multigenerational wealth. The core of the home was built in the mid 1800s, and has been renovated and expanded on by a long line of affluent owners, the last of whom being my late husband.

Everyone knows about the mansion, as well as the widow who now inhabits it. Both somewhat notorious, I suppose.

Grabbing the door frame for support, I toe-heel out of my boots, now caked in mud, and step into the kitchen.

Coffee, coffee, coffee.

Loudly and clumsily, I make my way around the marble island and somehow manage to set a pot.

For a moment, I panic, worried that my fiancé might

drop in for a late lunch and see me in this unattractive state. But as quickly as the thought enters my mind, it vanishes.

While waiting for the coffee to brew, I grab a loaf of bread from the pantry and begin stuffing torn pieces into my mouth like a gorilla, gumming the soft, springy center, and ignoring the pieces of crust that fall to the floor.

Soak up the booze, soak up the booze.

I squint at the calendar tacked up above the coffeepot, scanning my list of upcoming appointments.

Yep, I'm late.

I read the name attached to the appointment and my stomach drops to my feet.

Shit. I *can't* be late for this one.

The pot spits and gurgles, closing in on the end of its cycle.

I find my lucky mug in the dishwasher (that I forgot to run). Betty White's face smiles up at me, her middle finger raised to the sky. I grin. God bless Betty White. After half-heartedly rinsing the mug under the faucet, I fill it with coffee, splashing a puddle onto the counter.

Sobriety in hand, I make my way to the bedroom, my favorite room of the house. Floor-to-ceiling windows frame rolling mountains to the east, and to the west, rocky outcrops that lead to the ocean. A massive four-poster bed is the focal point of the room with a stone fireplace opposite it. Beyond the arched door is a marble bathroom and walk-in closet made for a queen—a princess, I should say.

I change into a white Donna Karan pantsuit while chugging the rest of the coffee—an extremely dangerous combination. Pull back my hair, slap on some makeup, and by the time I am slipping into my Louboutin heels, I am sober enough.

I stare at my reflection in the mirror.

Dr. Abbott, Dr. Abbott. You are *a doctor. You are smart, funny, and successful. You are a doctor. Smart, funny, and successful.*

After repeating the mantra several times, I make my way downstairs, then further still, into the basement. The large open space serves as my home office, a discreet counseling clinic for the Weeping Pines pocket crazies. A pocket crazy is someone who is a little deranged and a lot embarrassed about it. Someone who does not want to go to a traditional clinic for fear of being labeled by the town gossips.

I certainly understand that.

5

BETTS

*T*he clinic—no official name, just "the clinic"—came about organically, really. A way for me to make easy money.

After Jack died, I quit my job as the school counselor which I hated, but found myself, well, bored. At age thirty-seven, I was alone, a stranger in a sleepy logging town with a thriving population of just over fifteen hundred. I had no friends and was as welcome as a stray dog covered in mange.

One day, while grocery shopping, a disheveled mess of a woman ran up to me, a screaming toddler on one hip, a scowling preteen next to the other. She recognized me as the former school counselor.

"Dr. Betts, oh, Doctor, I called the school to schedule an appointment for my son, but they told me you'd left. I was really hoping you could talk to him."

Clutching a box of Monistat in one hand and a bottle of wine in the other, I glanced at the boy—greasy hair, sweaty armpits, a vile "me-against-the-world" expression on his face. Puberty at its finest.

"I'm sorry," I said, "but yes, that's right, I left my job a few weeks ago. Have they not hired another counselor?"

"Oh, that's right—I'm sorry to hear about your husband. But, no, they haven't hired another counselor. Not yet." The woman leans in, lowering her voice while ignoring the toddler punching the side of her face. "We—my husband and I—are going through a messy divorce, and Jimmy isn't taking it well. I'm really worried about him."

I wasn't surprised. Shortly after moving to Weeping Pines, I realized that it isn't only the Southern states that scorn divorce. It is every small town in America. Nobody divorces. Voluntarily breaking the bond of marriage is only marginally less sinful than cold-blooded murder. And even that's debatable.

I had hoped I had escaped this small-minded thinking when I left Arkansas. Nope. All small towns are the same— miserable housewives married to cheating husbands with mediocre incomes and even more mediocre personalities.

"Is there any way you can see him?" the woman asks. "Like, soon? Today? I'll pay cash."

I felt bad for her. And also, I like money.

"Sure, yes. I can do that." Of course I could. Easy work that would pay the bills while I slaved away on my sci-fi/young-adult something that would catapult me to instant fame. "How about we meet at the city park? Give me an hour?"

"Oh, that would be perfect."

A few days later, I received a call from the disheveled woman's sister who'd heard I'd opened "a clinic." I went with it. Told her I charged a hundred bucks an hour. Tori Card was sitting on my sofa an hour later.

I was online shopping an hour after that.

Then, word of mouth spread, and literally, just like that,

I, Dr. Abbott, the widow of Weeping Pines, opened an illegal counseling clinic in the basement of my late husband's home.

My "clinic" is not registered or insured. My "clients" pay in cash, cash that I fail to report to the IRS. I could very easily change this, fill out the paperwork to create an LLC, pay a measly yearly fee along with taxes. I just don't want to. I despise red tape almost as much as giving the government my hard-earned money.

Within a few months, I was making enough money to live on and avoid tapping into my savings. This made me happy. I was also no longer bored.

And this made me the happiest of all.

6

BETTS

I had just settled in behind my desk, feeling much less drunk, when the basement door opens.

Because of the way the basement was originally designed, the door is at ground level, above the basement, and therefore the low ceiling prevents me from seeing whoever enters through it. Six stone steps lead from the door into the basement. I don't like this and have considered a full redesign, but haven't taken the initiative to get it done.

The renovation Jack and I had undergone to turn the space into an office was costly enough, but worth it. Dark cherrywood floors run underneath expansive Persian rugs. Built-in bookshelves line the walls against beautiful wood paneling. Some are filled with books, others with expensive crystal decor pieces. The color palette is dark, earthy tones and dim lighting to allow for a relaxing spa-like atmosphere.

My desk sits in the middle, facing the outside door, a couch in front of it, facing me.

Her presence is announced by the *tap, tap, tap* of heels down the steps. Slow, confident, as if she has all the time in the world.

She probably does.

A sizzle of resentment, annoyance, rushes through my vodka-and-coffee-filled veins.

You are a doctor. She is not, I remind myself. *You are a doctor.* You *are a big deal.*

Inhaling, I pull back my shoulders and lift my chin as she slowly reveals herself one step at a time.

First, a pair of freshly manicured red toenails and peep-toe heels. Next, a pair of faded skinny jeans with the beginning of a rip in the knee, the quintessential "cool kid" jeans. This followed by a vintage Janis Joplin T-shirt underneath an oversized cardigan.

Long black hair slowly reveals itself, and then finally, her face. The face of an angel. Exotic olive-toned skin, dark almond-shaped eyes, a thin nose, and for the cherry on top, big ol' fuck-me lips.

Carmen Marquis looks like a Victoria's Secret model. Not one of the bombshell blondes but rather one of the mysterious black-haired, come-hither sirens. The kind of beauty you watch from across the room. She is that kind of woman.

A Weeping Pines native, Carmen has recently returned to her hometown after leaving Los Angeles where she lived for over a decade. There, she'd dropped out of college and published eight romantic-suspense novels, becoming a best-selling and award-winning author by age twenty-five. She and I are kindred spirits in that manner. Although, apparently, writing comes much easier to her than to me.

Anyway, after Carmen's last bestseller, she stopped writing and dropped off the face of the earth. No one knows why. She is now thirty-one. It is a bit of a mystery why she returned home. She has no husband, no kids, no boyfriend, is a vegetarian and a Food Network addict.

She is also a woman with severe anger issues.

That's right. This Victoria's Secret model has a serious case of rage and regret. Carmen likes to break things. This is the root of her coming to me—or to my clinic, I should say.

The story goes like this:

Carmen's old high school boyfriend—Chris or Chet, I can't remember—allowed her to temporarily crash on his couch when she moved back from LA. Soon after, the cops responded to a domestic disturbance call at the residence, where she had reportedly hit him over the head with a mayonnaise jar during an argument.

Chris (or Chet) decided to drop charges after being chided by his friends for not being able to control "his woman." WPPD happily closed the case and recommended that Carmen seek therapeutic treatment for her anger. She did, twice, but then quit going.

Rumor is, Carmen didn't get along with the local therapist, Dr. Hahn, a seventy-three-year-old German man with a curious obsession with buttons. Hahn's office walls are covered in buttons—in frames, on swatches of fabric, in clocks, as table and chair accents. Even the newsboy cap he wears every day is covered in buttons. Anyway, she quit seeing him, and this is when she found me and my secret underground clinic.

During the first few visits, it was obvious Carmen was guarded and reluctant. Some days, I wondered if she had rehearsed a script before coming to see me, just to fill the dead air. After every visit, I expected to never see her again. Yet she continues to show up, going on five months now.

Carmen Marquis is my favorite client. She is also the one I despise the most. A juxtaposition that makes her, quite frankly, extremely interesting to me.

She and I have talked about everything from global

warming to gun control, from home remedies for yeast infections to her favorite kind of hot sauce. We've spent hours—literally—debating the pros and cons of self-publishing versus traditional publishing. Hours of one-on-one conversations, and we still hadn't gotten to the root of her anger issues.

Five months, and we are still skimming above the surface, yet to delve into anything deep or worthy enough of psychiatric evaluation.

This appointment begins as they usually do, with small talk. We discuss the weather. I ask if she's lost weight, remembering we discussed a fad diet during her last appointment. No, she says. An awkward beat passes between us, then another failed conversation starter. Blah, blah, blah, me sipping coffee between every question, trying to ward off the post-vodka headache that is creeping up.

I clear my throat and refocus.

"I saw the beautiful pictures you posted of the last few sunrises," I say, forcing a smile.

I also saw the pictures of her tits spilling out of her low-cut shirt as she stared reflectively at the ocean, a glass of wine in one hand, her own book in the other. A shameless plug, a dirty marketing trick. Stop scrolling to look at my boobs, and oh yeah, go buy the book I'm holding in my hand.

Carmen Marquis is a pro at creating social media clickbait.

This kind of self-indulgence makes me want to vomit.

I spent days, weeks even, trying to find my perfect angle on social media. I bought a selfie stick, a selfie stand, a selfie stand with a fancy illumination ring. I downloaded an app promising to smooth my skin and make my face appear "perfect." Nothing worked. The Gadleigh Estate makes for a great backdrop, but it's nothing compared to Carmen's newly purchased clifftop cottage overlooking the Pacific Ocean.

Carmen posts in the morning, at lunch, and in the evening, and sometimes, if I'm lucky, in the middle of the night.

It isn't until about twenty minutes into our session that I notice the fuzz of a white bandage peeking out of her sleeve. Any psychologist knows that seeing a bandage around your patient's wrist is an immediate red flag. Your doctor instincts pique, ringing loudly like a tornado warning in a small town. I make a point not to stare at the bandage, and then deftly maneuver the conversation to align with this new, very concerning development.

"Talk to me about your last few days, Carmen. How were they? Good, bad?"

"You're asking what I did?"

"Yeah. Don't overthink it. Just talk about your last few days."

"Okay, well, I'm on a tight deadline for my next book, so I've been focusing on that."

"Ah. You didn't mention you were getting back into writing."

"What makes you think I stopped?"

"You haven't published a book in a while, right?"

"Four years."

Three years and four months to be exact, but who's counting?

"You've been writing this entire time?" I ask, and I find myself wanting to tell her that I am writing a book too. But then remember I am a nobody in this world of publishing. Best not bring attention to that fact.

"Here and there," she says.

"Why'd you stop publishing?"

Carmen looks away, and I sense there is a lot to unpack in this subject. It's not hard to imagine that the story has dark edges. After all, the woman published a book every six months, gained national success. Then, at what seemed to be the peak of her career, she suddenly went MIA, only to show up back in her miserable hometown with a penchant for mayonnaise jars.

"Carmen?"

Our eyes meet, and her message is clear. She doesn't want to talk about this topic.

I don't force it because there are more pressing matters to get to, like the bandage around her wrist.

"What is this particular book about?" I ask.

She shifts and crosses her impossibly long legs. "Do you remember that story from years ago about the bored housewife who poisoned her husband with eye drops?"

I sit up straighter. "Yes, I think so . . . the Visine murder or something like that. It was big news for a while, right?"

"Right. I want to build a character around her. Do you know her husband suffered for three days? Three days, the woman watched her husband dying. Three days, and never once did she have a moment of 'Oh my God, I need to save him.' Crazy, isn't it? I'm trying to build a picture of why she would do something that extreme. I mean, why not just shoot him in the head? I also read that a few months earlier, she tried to poison him with nightshade—you know, those toxic little blue berries that look just like blueberries. He didn't eat enough and just got sick. Never knew it was her. Anyway, I've read everything I can on the case and on her, specifically."

"And what have you gathered so far?"

Carmen looks thoughtfully up at the ceiling, chewing on her lower lip. "That's the thing—she was pretty normal. A nurse, nothing really to talk about. There were all sorts of allegations about their marriage, but nothing was proven."

I smile. "Looks like you're going to need a twist to make her more interesting for a main character."

"Exactly." Carmen gives me a smile back, but just as quickly, her face falls again. "I just . . . I can't seem to find the trigger of it all."

"Did you get the court records or transcripts?"

"Only what's online."

"Any implication of weird childhood behaviors?"

"No, nothing proven."

"What about self-harm? Cutting, perhaps? Any history there?"

Her dark eyes slowly narrow. "You're talking about the Band-Aids around my wrist."

"Yes, Carmen, I am."

"Why didn't you just ask me directly? Ask me if I'm a cutter?"

"I understand this can be a very delicate topic. I wanted to give you the opportunity to evade."

"I see."

"So?"

"So, it was an accident."

"What kind of accident?"

"Your fault, really."

"My fault?"

"Yes. I decided to try out your suggestion. Breaking things in a controlled, safe manner."

"Did you?" My brow cocks. "Well, I'm not sure if I should say *good job* or *I'm sorry*. How did you do it?"

"I've been doing a bit of pruning in my yard, getting ready for the fall season . . ." *Pruning.* The word sounds so important and pretentious from her lips. ". . . and there was a large rotting limb on the edge of my property. I decided to chop it."

"Just chop it up, huh?"

"Yes, for firewood, for the winter."

"Is this how you hurt your wrist?"

"Yes."

A moment passes as we stare at each other. Will I press further? Or will she tell me what *really* happened?

"Talk to me about how you felt when you chopped this wood." I wrap my hands around my empty coffee mug.

"It hurt."

"No, I mean psychologically."

"Oh. Better."

"Better is good. Was there a trigger that made you decide to try my idea of breaking something in a controlled manner? Did someone make you mad?"

"Someone always makes me mad."

"Who made you mad that day?"

"The FedEx guy."

"What did the FedEx guy do?"

"Didn't leave a box on my doorstep as he was supposed to do."

"Let me guess—a box that required a signature."

She rolls her eyes. "I was on the deck, working. I didn't hear him knock. Next thing I know, there's a piece of paper taped to my door that says *sorry I missed you.*"

"I understand that can be frustrating."

"No, Dr. Betts, frustrating is when your $4,000 laptop suddenly freezes, you lose all your files, and have to send it off for repair while you are on a deadline."

"Did you have a backup of the files?"

"Do you have something I can break in a controlled manner?"

"I'll take that as a no." I grin. Carmen is kind of funny. "Okay, so you got mad and decided to chop wood instead of chasing down the driver and busting him over the head with a mayonnaise jar."

"That's the fourth time you've made that joke since I started coming here."

"It doesn't get old."

"I strongly disagree."

"Why a mayonnaise jar?" I shake my head. "You're a writer. It should have been something more interesting."

"I was making a sandwich when we started arguing."

"What kind of sandwich?"

"I'm not paying you a hundred dollars an hour to discuss sandwiches."

"No, you're paying me to understand the root of your aggression so that you don't end up in jail for not being able to control your anger."

"Tofu. I was making a faux-turkey sandwich when my idiot roommate started accusing me of banging his best friend. I wasn't."

I'm careful to keep my expression in check. It's not hard to imagine Carmen having multiple relationships at the same time.

"The argument escalated," she opens her palms, "and the rest is Weeping Pines history."

"So . . ." I fold my hands on the table. "As we spoke about last week, the psychological reason behind people punching or breaking things when they're mad is simple, really. It offers an immediate release of tension. More than that, if you hit something hard enough, it can also physically exhaust you, forcing your body to relax. So, you hitting your roommate—or *boyfriend*, not my business—in the head with a jar released the anger you were feeling inside. You chopping firewood released the anger you were feeling toward the FedEx guy. It's important to acknowledge this. To realize that there is a release, that you are capable of controlling it."

I pull in a breath. "But the key here, Carmen, is that punching a wall, chopping wood, or throwing objects isn't really a solution. While it may help you in the immediate moment with a cathartic release of stress, nothing really changes in terms of your anger management issues. It is literally giving in to them. Remember, our goal here is to get to the root of your anger issues and fix it at its very core. So you no longer feel the need to punch anything."

Her gaze shifts to the single photo I keep on my desk. It is a five-by-seven of me and my fiancé on vacation in Hawaii, the evening he asked me to marry him.

"So, in that vein," I say, increasing my volume to redirect her, "let's loop back to my original question about what led up to you feeling like you needed to chop wood."

"The FedEx guy."

"It wasn't just the FedEx guy, Carmen."

Her attention returns to me. "I don't know. I guess the stress of my deadline. I've been waking up in the middle of the night. I can't shut my mind off, so I get up and work."

"That can't be healthy. When do you sleep?"

"During the day, mostly. Often on the couch."

I lean forward. "Carmen, take it from me, when someone doesn't get enough sleep, they're angry whether they have anger issues or not."

"Get more sleep. Got it, Doc."

Again, she momentarily considers the picture of my fiancé.

Our eyes meet. Perhaps it was the lingering haze of the vodka or the buzz of the coffee, but something passes between us. Something unspoken that makes me pause, something that makes me *feel*.

The sound of tires comes up the driveway. I have no appointments after this, and I am not expecting any guests.

"Excuse me." I push away from my desk and cross the room, feeling Carmen's gaze following me.

Insecurity sweeps through me. I need to lose ten pounds, fifteen even. I take the stairs that lead into the house and close the door quietly behind me. I tiptoe down the hall and peek out the window.

It's not just any vehicle. This unannounced visitor is arriving in a WPPD cop car.

My stomach rolls.

I stand frozen for a minute, my brain short-circuiting.

Why would the cops be visiting me? Perhaps my secret (illegal) clinic is not so secret anymore.

I spin around. Carmen needs to leave or hide. Something.

My heart pounding, I jog down the hall and into the basement.

But Carmen is gone.

7

BETTS

"Good afternoon, Miss Abbott."

"Good afternoon."

I cringe at the trepidation in my tone, and in my behavior, for that matter. I am peeking through the door like a teenager warned to never open the door to strangers.

Except this man is no stranger.

Detective Nicholas Stahl gives me that cocky smile of his, taking me in, allowing for a stretch of awkward silence.

He always does this. It reminds me of the old Colombo show—you remember Nick at Nite?—where the goofy main character, a detective, asks stupid questions and appears oblivious to everything. But in the end, his aloof nature was all just a brilliant act to catch the criminal. Colombo always wins.

I cannot say the same for Detective Nicholas Stahl.

I quickly scan the driveway. Carmen usually parks her Tahoe behind the house, close to the basement entrance. So, from my vantage point, I can't see if her vehicle is gone or not.

Where the hell did she go? Bathroom, maybe?

"How can I help you?" I open the door wider, practicing my own aloof expression. Stahl's body fills the doorway. At a thick six-foot-three, the man is an intimidating presence, I'll give him that. "Is everything okay?"

"Oh yes, yes." He glances over my shoulder, into the house, as he allows another beat of an awkward pause.

Stahl is wearing an off-duty uniform, a WPPD T-shirt tucked into khaki tactical pants and brown combat boots. I notice the circles under his dark eyes and the beginnings of crow's feet, a fatigue I've never seen before in the usually spry busybody.

Meeting my eyes again, he says, "I just came by to express my condolences for the loss of your mother last week."

I blink. "Thank you."

"She died of a heart attack, yes?"

"Yes. She had heart disease for a long time before she passed."

"I'm sorry to hear that." His attention slips from my eyes and slowly sweeps me from head to toe. "You look nice."

I glance down at the white pantsuit, wildly inappropriate for an afternoon at home. But, then again, what I choose to wear in my home is none of his damned business.

Refusing to take the bait, I lift my chin. He probably thinks I have a date. Good. I couldn't care less.

Stahl glances again over my shoulder. "The place looks great. You've had the crown molding replaced since I last stopped by."

"Yes."

"And added wood paneling. What is that? Pine?"

Jesus Christ, Colombo.

"I'm not sure what kind of wood it is."

"Mind if I take a look? I'm thinking about getting paneling for my entryway."

Where the hell is Carmen?

"Sure, come on in, Nicholas." I hold my breath as he passes, hoping he won't detect the stale scent of liquor lingering on my breath.

After closing the door, I turn. Stahl is standing in the middle of the hallway, staring at me, not my wood paneling.

I gesture to the wall. "Well. There it is."

Stahl turns to the wood, studying each piece with the scrutiny of an airport security agent. "Yep, looks like it's pine."

I shrug. "Okay." *Whatever.*

"Who did it for you?"

"I'll have to look. I hired a contractor to handle it. Paul something."

"Paul Simpson."

"Yep." I flick a finger in a *bingo* sort of way. "That's the guy."

The detective nods, approving of this decision. "I know him well. We volunteered together at the fire station a few years ago."

"Cool."

"Did he only do paneling for you?"

"No, he did a few other things too—I actually renovated the master bathroom."

"The bathroom." Stahl tilts his head back with a chuckle. "Well, I'll try not to be offended. Do you know how many weekends I spent working on that very bathroom during my teenage years? Blood, sweat, and tears right there in that bathroom you renovated."

"Oh, sorry. I just wanted to add a Jacuzzi tub."

"No, no, no, I'm not offended. I know it was a bit dated.

But you know Jack, he always liked the traditional aesthetic. Authentic. Organic. Can I see it?"

"See what?"

"The bathroom."

I glance at my wristwatch for no other reason than to ensure Stahl is certain that he is unwelcome.

"Sure . . . right this way."

Born and raised in Weeping Pines, Nicholas is somewhat of a staple in town. A local-hero kind of man. He is well known—attractive single men usually are—mostly in part to my late husband, Jack, who hired Nicholas during his young impressionable teenage years to help renovate the Gadleigh Estate, long before Jack and I ever met. This led to a decades-long friendship and mentorship.

The story goes that Nicholas had a notoriously rough childhood—neglect, abuse, the works—and Jack took Nicholas under his wing, even allowing Nicholas to live in the mansion for a short time. Eventually, Jack became somewhat of a godfather to the wayward teen.

Despite Nicholas and me being close in age, I never liked the guy. I'm not exactly sure why. Perhaps because he never liked me. From the moment Jack introduced us, Nicholas regarded me in a way that suggested I was undeserving of the situation I had found myself in. I wasn't good enough for the man he idolized.

This amused me. Jack was well off, and yes, I was fifteen years his junior, but it wasn't like he was sitting on tens of millions of dollars for me to spend on shoes and handbags. Jack was no better than me, and vice versa. I didn't marry Jack for his money—we married because we loved each other. We were a team, one that no longer included Nicholas, which I assumed was the issue.

After Jack died, it was revealed that Nicholas, his unofficial godson, had been left out of his will. This was big town gossip, surprising even me. This should have been the end of Nicholas in my life.

It wasn't.

He continued to drop by the Gadleigh Estate, uninvited and unannounced, even after Jack died. Just like he is now.

To be honest, sometimes it creeps me out a bit.

Stahl follows me down the hall, through the living room, where the television has been on since I wandered out to the picnic table with a pint of vodka hours earlier. I grab the remote and click it off the Food Network as we pass. Finally, we reach the master bedroom that takes up almost half of the first floor.

"Wow." He lets out a whistle and stuffs his hands in his pants pockets. "It's so different."

"Yeah, I changed it up a bit."

"Too hard to deal with the memories?"

I stare straight ahead. "Yes, something like that."

Stahl nods, then slowly scans the room. "When my mom died, my dad did the same thing. Rearranged every piece of furniture in the house. Was too difficult to live in the house without her. As it was, anyway."

I frown, mentally reaching back in my hazy memory. I am pretty sure Jack told me Nicholas's parents died together of a drug overdose.

Whatever. I don't care.

Stahl steps into the bathroom. "Wow, this looks amazing. Paul sure does do good work."

"Thanks. And yes, he does. He also charges an arm and a leg for it."

The detective studies the marble counter, the mirrored plate of expensive perfumes. He lingers on the small crystal butterfly in the center.

"That's beautiful. Did your mom get it for you?"

"No."

"Looks like something a mom would get her daughter."

He obviously never met my mother.

"You didn't have a funeral for her, correct?"

I shift my weight, edging closer to the door. "That's right. Well, not a big one, anyway. I did a small thing with some of our close friends down in Arkansas."

"At Hilltop Cemetery, right?"

Nerves bubble in my stomach. "That's right."

Stahl nods, lingering again on the glass butterfly, a bullshit tchotchke I purchased on a whim at one of the eclectic shops downtown.

"Thought it was interesting," he says, turning to me.

"What was interesting?"

"That you had her buried."

"Detective, you might be the only person on the planet who considers having a deceased person buried interesting."

He laughs. "Blame it on the day job. No, I meant, interesting that you didn't have her cremated."

The little synapses in my brain begin to short circuit.

"You know, because you were so adamant about having Jack cremated." Stahl pauses. "You know . . . unsuccessfully, since his will clearly stated that he wanted to be buried."

The detective claps his hands together, sending my heart leaping into my throat.

"Welp, I don't want to take any more of your time," he says, then breezes past me.

I'm still confused as we fall into step together down the hallway and into the living room.

"I think I'll reach out to Paul about that wood paneling,"

Stahl says, opening the door. "It's exactly what I'm looking for."

We step outside and exchange pleasant farewells.

As I watch Detective Stahl drive down my driveway, I wonder exactly what he had been trying to find. Because it definitely had nothing to do with wood paneling.

8

BETTS

I am slaving away on my sci-fi/young-adult manuscript when I hear the grind of the garage door. My jaw clenches and shoulders tense. Unfortunately, this has become my body's automatic response to my fiancé's arrival.

I shove the pen and notebook in a drawer and scan the dinner table. The plates are in their correct spots, knives and forks positioned perfectly in the center of each napkin. A glass of water sits next to an empty wineglass—which I must not fill until he is seated. A freshly chopped salad sits next to the salt and pepper shakers. The lasagna is cooling on the stove, the garlic bread next to it, the empty pint of vodka I drank earlier nowhere in sight.

The door opens.

I quickly push away my wine, as if I'd only recently poured it and am not certain if I even want it or not. Then I face the doorway and smile like a faithful soldier, a servant patiently waiting for their master.

Ian doesn't greet me in the kitchen as he usually does. Instead, his footsteps turn toward the bedroom.

I take a deep swallow of my wine, then set it down. Stare at the doorway.

Wait.

And wait.

Seven minutes later, Ian emerges from the bedroom where he shed his slacks and dress shirt and is now wearing a pair of baggy basketball shorts and a long-sleeve T-shirt. He is flipping through a stack of mail as he steps into the kitchen.

"Hey."

My fiancé turns from the stack, forcing a smile that doesn't quite reach his pale blue eyes. "Hey, you."

Returning to the solicitations, he slides into his seat at the head of the table.

I tilt my head to the side, taking in the man who is more interested in a discount flyer than the woman he asked to marry him two years ago.

He is white, my fiancé. I'm not talking ethnically; I'm talking literally. The skin on my fiancé's body is only a shade paler than his hair. His hair is not gray—Ian is only forty-two—but so blond it is almost translucent. Even his eyes lack pigment. He is not albino (I asked), just very pale. And in an ironic twist, Ian's favorite color to wear is—you guessed it—white.

Despite all this, Ian is a handsome man, in a vampire surfer-boy kind of way.

"Have you heard about this place?" He holds a flyer in his hand.

"No, what's it called?" I remove the clear wrap from the salad bowl. I don't bother with the sexy "lean-over-the-table-and-show-my-cleavage" move I practiced twenty minutes earlier.

"Sally's Home Cooking. It's a food-delivery service. Says they only do low-carb, keto, organic dishes."

I glance at the lasagna cooling on the stove as he continues.

"We should try it," he says.

I down the rest of my wine.

Ian Bailey is the town dentist. The second dentist, I should say. Sparkling Smiles, a large regional dentistry, is the main (preferred) clinic. Smiles, as everyone calls them, put down roots in Weeping Pines over twenty years ago and has since scooped up ninety percent of the market. The other ten percent belongs to Ian's father's practice, Bailey Dentistry. After Ian's father retired and moved to Arizona, Ian took over the practice with the goal to revive and "modernize" it, and eventually expand operations.

This is where I met him, several years ago. I had an abscessed tooth. This posed a problem because I had sworn off going in public until the gossip about our marriage died down. So, instead of calling Smiles, the dentistry where Jack was a client, I decided to try out the smaller clinic on the town square.

I left Bailey Dentistry with a prescription for painkillers and a telephone number. Although we'd known each other for a while, after Jack died Ian's fervor increased. He wined and dined me, the most recent widow of Weeping Pines, the inheritor of the Gadleigh Estate and more than a million dollars from my late husband's life insurance policy.

Ian was different from Jack. Where Jack had been a challenge, Ian had shamelessly swept me off my feet. Old school, you know? Flowers, opening doors, pulling out chairs. He even ordered for me once at a restaurant.

I liked the way he made me feel. He made me laugh. Made me feel wanted. I also liked the feeling of being financially stable in my own right. I was the one with the money, for a change. I had the upper hand. I felt powerful. Confident.

Six months later, Ian Bailey asked me to marry him at sunset on the beach in Hawaii. A picnic dinner with champagne, artisan sandwiches, fancy desserts, and one massive diamond ring in the bottom of the basket.

I said yes. Why? Because that's what you say when the man you love asks you to marry him on the beach. Everything else can be worked out later. Or not worked out, for that matter.

Two months after that, I learned Bailey Dentistry was one bad check away from filing bankruptcy. To no one's surprise, the small LLC was unable to compete with the cutthroat pricing and advanced technology of a regional chain.

I gave my fiancé a "loan" to keep his business afloat.

I shouldn't have.

"How was your day," I ask, refilling my wineglass.

Ian glances at the bottle, then at me. "It was busy. What's for dinner?"

"I made lasagna, extra carbs."

"Smells great," he says, ignoring the dig.

Smart.

I plate the pasta, the salad, and the bread, then slide it in front of him. Fill his glass.

He waits until I am seated with my own plate to take a bite. "Delicious. Good job."

I smile. It's Marie Callender's, right out of the freezer section of the grocery store. I can only hope Ian is better at spotting cavities than fake homemade dinners.

As usual, we pick at our plates, Ian waiting for his buzz

to kick in before indulging me in his predictable list of questions about my day.

Tonight, however, he surprises me. "Did Carmen Marquis come by and see you today?"

I blink. "Yes, she did. How did you know that?"

"I saw it on your schedule."

I glance at the calendar above the coffeepot. Ian is fully aware of the legal complications of my clinic, but he doesn't address it. How could he? I'm funding his business. He has no room to criticize me. But this isn't what I am concerned about right now.

"Do you know Carmen?" I ask.

"She came in once."

"Came in where?"

"My clinic."

"For what?"

"A cleaning."

"Just once?"

"Yeah."

"When?"

"Why?"

"Just curious."

"A few months ago, I guess. You're being weird."

I chase a piece of burned pasta with my fork. I am being weird.

Shut up, Betts, shut up.

Ian forks up another bite. "I heard she's got a new book coming out."

The only way my fiancé would know this information is if he had spoken to Carmen recently, because there is nothing about the book on her social media. I should know . . . I scrolled her feed only five minutes earlier.

My pulse picks up speed, as it does when I realize I am on the cusp of a new journey—good or bad.

"Yes, she's struggling with her deadline," I say coolly. "That was the bulk of our conversation today."

He nods and shoves a forkful of lasagna in his mouth.

A minute passes.

"Are you taking your medicine?" he asks.

"Yes."

"Are you?" He swallows, narrowing his eyes at me.

"Yes, I promise."

"Well, I was at the pharmacy today, and Carl mentioned you have an overdue prescription to be filled."

"What business is that of Carl's?"

"We're engaged. Everyone knows."

"And everyone knows that prescription accounts are to be private, regardless of your marital status. That's incredibly unprofessional—"

"You're deflecting."

Heat rises up my neck. "I am taking them."

"Okay, good, because you know what happens—"

"I am taking them, and I am also done with this conversation."

Ian pops a brow, shrugs, and focuses on his dinner.

We eat in silence. All I can think about is when and where he saw Carmen Marquis. How did he know about her new book?

I'm mad. I can feel the anger brewing like a storm in my stomach. I'm drunk too. And despite the little voice in my head telling me to keep my mouth shut, I decide to light this dinner on fire.

"Detective Stahl came by this afternoon."

Ian's fork freezes in mid-air as he scrutinizes me. "Again?"

I thrill at his visceral response but keep my emotions in check. "Yes."

Ian drops his fork, his throat working in a deep swallow. "Why this time?"

"He came by to offer his condolences for my mother's passing."

Ian barks out a laugh. A small piece of pasta flies out and sticks to his chin, but I don't tell him. "Did he?"

"Yes."

"Why?"

"I just told you—to offer his condolences for my mother's death.

"No, I mean *why*. Did he somehow know your mother in Arkansas?"

"No—"

"So, really, it was to console *you*."

"Is this a problem?"

"*He* is a problem. I can't stand the guy; you know that. He never comes by when I'm here, do you notice that? He's obsessed with you, Betts, I'm telling you."

I want to laugh. I want to dance. Laugh at how wrong Ian is, and dance at the victory I feel from his possessive response.

"He's never let go," Ian says. "It's weird."

"Well, Jack was very important to him."

"No, Betts, of you. He's never let go of you. Of . . . the thing."

I blink, my eyes rounding as we stare at each other.

The thing.

Ian has never mentioned it before now, and we've never spoken of it.

The thing between us.

9

BETTS

The night may be bitter cold, but it's warmer than air in the house. I can't take the tension between Ian and me another second, so I decide to go for a walk after cleaning up dinner.

I quietly close the door and then wrap my neck in a thick wool scarf. My breath comes out in puffs as I cross the backyard.

The bulb on the outdoor security light flickers as I pass by, washing the trees in a sickly yellow glow. Beyond that, pitch darkness. Not a single star in the sky tonight.

I step into the woods.

Head down, shoulders hunched, I walk the path I've trodden countless times before. I could do it with my eyes shut.

The picnic table is covered in wet leaves, recently discarded from the surrounding trees. I climb to the top of the table and sit, my boots resting on the bench.

The night is quiet, and so black, it's as if you can reach out and grab it.

I stare through the trees at the home I inherited from my

late husband. It seems even larger in the night, each end marked by dots of lamplight in random rooms.

I reminisce on my first week here, when sleep evaded me and I spent each night pacing the floor. From one end of the place to the other, pivot, repeat. Hundreds of laps around my new house, watching the clock tick as each minute passed. It was supposed to be my forever home, a notion that should have felt comforting and exciting. Instead, it felt disconcerting.

As with any old home, especially one that's like a medieval castle, rumors of otherworldly incidents plagued the house, along with whispers that whoever crossed its door was cursed forever.

Depending on who you ask, the Gadleigh Estate is haunted. There are many legends, but most notably, two. One includes a woman, the long-ago lady of the house, found by her husband lying in bed with her eyes gouged out and her tongue cut off. Her name was Alexandria Quiten. The mystery went unsolved. Rumor is, she still walks the halls today, waiting for her killer to be caught.

The other, and most widely known story, is the haunting of four children, said to have been locked in the attic and brutally tortured by their mentally ill parents before eventually perishing. Legend says the spirits of the four children still live in the attic, this vouched for by several construction workers, groundskeepers, and housekeepers who have claimed to have either seen or heard them over the years. More than a dozen sightings of these mysterious children have been recorded.

I've never—not once—gone into the attic. And I don't care to. *Ever.*

I think about them, though, those kids. Sometimes I wonder if they have communicated with the three that died in my belly. Are they here? Little half-formed beings running amok with the other child spirits, laughing at me and my inability to grow them correctly? Do they conspire against me—the body that killed them? Or do they look at me with envy, a fully formed human that they will never become?

I am pondering this thought, once again, when my attention is pulled to the sound of a twig popping somewhere behind me. A chill flies up my spine, and over my shoulder I see nothing but blackness.

I freeze in place, knowing that I am in the dark and therefore whoever—or whatever—can't see me. This also means I can't see them.

I hold my breath and strain to listen, but all I can hear is the blood rushing through my ears.

One second passes, ten, twenty. A minute.

I begin to relax and convince myself the sound came from a squirrel harvesting nuts. Regardless, I am a bit creeped out and decide that I want to go home.

As I shift to move off the picnic table, a figure steps out from behind a tree, backlit by the outdoor security light. It stands directly between me and the house, and stares at me.

I stare back, completely frozen in fear.

"Hello," I call out, my voice shaking. "This is private property."

It isn't the first time I've found a wayward hiker on my land, especially this time of year. But never at this time of night.

The silhouette doesn't respond.

"I have a gun," I shout, lying.

Still, nothing.

I slowly climb off the picnic table and stand tall in a ridiculous display of confidence.

A loud pop comes from behind me, sending me whirling around, my heart leaping into my throat. I hear the thud of a broken tree branch fall to the ground.

When I turn back, the figure is gone.

I exhale, and for a second, wonder if I imagined it.

As I hurry through the woods, my eyes locked on the house, I can't help but think of the last dead body I saw in it.

10

BETTS

*O*nce I am certain no one is lurking outside the house, I carry a bottle of wine to the bedroom.

Ian has slunk away to the den to catch Monday night football. I don't know why. The man has never thrown a ball in his life. Soon, he will doze off on the recliner, where he will sleep until one or two in the morning. Then he will sneak into bed with me, where I will pretend to be asleep until my alarm goes off at six.

I change out of the fuck-me blouse that Ian didn't notice, and into a pair of baggy gray sweatpants and even baggier sweatshirt.

Bottle in hand, I disappear down into the basement. Ian's personal space is the den, and mine is the basement. Over the last three years, I have spent more time in this room under my house than officially inside it. It is my safe place. My place to just be me. Just be myself.

I check the window, searching one last time for the dark silhouette.

I imagined it. I must have.

I sink into the couch that faces my desk—the client

couch, I call it—in the exact spot Carmen perched hours earlier.

I can smell her. A sharp fruity scent that lingers long after she leaves the room. Backlist Cherry, the perfume is called. It took me three weeks and over a hundred dollars in samples until I found it.

It doesn't smell the same on me.

Mindlessly, I trail my finger along the leather where her arm rested.

Staring at the empty chair behind the desk, I try to picture myself there, sitting, listening, occasionally taking notes. How do I appear to my clients? What does Carmen see when she looks at me?

I make a mental note to add a lamp opposite the current one and replace the light bulbs. Dim, flattering light to illuminate whatever there is of me that's worthy of seeing.

I replay our appointment, the back and forth, the way she crossed her legs, the way she contemplated the photo of my fiancé.

I picture Ian's face as he asked about her during dinner. Dispassionately, but was it all a ruse?

I think of Detective Stahl and his odd visit.

I think of Jack.

My gaze shifts to the bookcase. As if being pulled by a magnet, I push off the couch, cross the room, and retrieve the large leather binder tucked between a travel book and a medical journal.

Slowly, I lower to the floor, crisscross my legs, set my wine next to me, and untie the leather strap that binds the folder. I begin carefully taking out the contents, my pulse slowly increasing with each piece.

I filter through the pictures of our wedding day, the event of the year in Weeping Pines, Jack's hometown. I looked so beautiful. My dress was designer, as were my shoes. The diamonds in my ears, around my neck, and on my fingers are real. A real fairy-tale moment.

And Jack was just as stunning, dashing in his black tuxedo. I remember the way he carried himself, his back pin straight, his head always held high. He had an aura of power, and I think this is what drew me to him in the first place. I was thirty-five when I married Jack Holden. He was fifty.

My Prince Charming.

I pull out a newspaper clipping. The headline reads:

MAN FOUND DEAD IN LOCAL HISTORIC MANSION

Below it is a black-and-white photo of our house, the Gadleigh Estate.

I read his obituary for the hundredth time.

Dr. Jack G. Holden, age 51, of Weeping Pines, was found dead Monday, October 29, 2018, at his home, the historic Gadleigh Estate.

Jack Gordon Holden was born July 15, 1967, at Northside Regional Hospital, to Gordon and Elsie Holden. He was raised in Weeping Pines and graduated with honors from Weeping Pines High School. Jack earned his MD in Neurology from Berkeley. Following his residency in Brookings, he joined Hats and Gull Medical Center in New York, where he worked until his retirement in 2017.

Jack married Betty Lou Abbott on June 9, 2017, at Cross Connection Church in Weeping Pines.

Jack was president of Hats and Gull Medical Center and past president of the medical staff of the Berkley Center for Neurology. Jack was a Fellow of the Mental Health and Substance Abuse Services, and of the Leadership and Education Advancement

Program for Diverse Scholars. Jack educated medical students and residents, and mentored physician assistants and nurse-practitioner students.

Jack served on the PCCO board of directors and as Madison Health Officer, New Beginnings Medical Advisor, and sat on the United Way board of directors. He was a member of Cross Connection Church. Jack was an avid runner and bicyclist.

Survivors include his wife, Betty Lou Abbott. Jack had no children. He was preceded in death by his parents.

Visitation begins at noon on Wednesday at Nelson Funeral Home and continues one hour prior to the service. Funeral services will be 11:00 a.m. Thursday at Nelson Funeral Home.

In lieu of flowers, the family asks that memorials be directed to Northside Regional Hospital, Cross Connection Church, or United Way.

Before I can stop myself, I drop my head in my hands and weep.

11

BETTS

Five years earlier: New York

Picture this: A young woman from Arkansas, a newly certified doctor of psychology, with her suitcase in one hand and the key to her first place in the other, a studio apartment in New York City.

She is young, eager, ready to take on the world. Nothing can stand in her way. She is going to be the next Carrie Bradshaw—but really, really smart. Her weekends will be spent in designer clothes, running around with her doctor friends, dating multiple men, and then gossiping about it over twenty-dollar martinis and tiny hors d'oeuvres.

She is me.

I'll never forget the day I officially left Arkansas and landed in the Big Apple. I felt like I had the entire world in the palm of my hand. And at that moment, I guess I did.

It was summer in New York, and I, Betty Lou Abbott, was attending my first medical convention, representing the team of Horizon Clinic, a mental health facility where I had secured a paid internship. Horizon specialized in cognitive behavior therapy for trust issues specifically. In a nutshell, my job was listening to bored housewives whine about their cheating husbands. In the first few months, I'd heard enough down-and-dirty gossip to fill a lifetime. And I loved every freaking second of it.

I'd bought a new skirt for the occasion. A long, pleated, high-waisted skirt that made me want to twirl in circles in the middle of the road. I paired this fantastic skirt with a silk blouse that draped like butter over my barely B-cups.

The convention was being held at the Grand Marquis on Times Square. Thousands of rooms, thousands of people bustling in and out. A twenty-four/seven beehive of noise and activity.

Briefcase in hand, I stepped onto the escalator that would carry me to the main level. I was watching a woman wrangle two unruly toddlers when I reached the top of the escalator. I stepped off. My skirt did not. The hem of it caught in the spinning metal teeth of the escalator and was being eaten alive, pulling me down with it.

I screamed and flung my briefcase into the air—literally. I could not have been more dramatic. People around me began to scream. Kids began to cry. Chaos ensued.

I yanked wildly at the skirt, trying to rip away the fabric, with no luck. At that point, I was certain that I was going to die. I was going to be sucked between the metal teeth and chopped into long spaghetti strands of flesh, never to be seen or heard of again.

All of a sudden, two big manly hands grabbed the end of my skirt and with one strong yank, ripped the fabric free from the metal monster. I flew backward, landing on my ass with my legs spread open. Thank God I'd shaved.

The escalator chose that very moment to stop. *Thanks a lot.*

I looked up into the eyes of the most beautiful man I had ever seen in my life. He was wearing a navy suit over a blinding-white shirt. Salt-and-pepper hair, perfectly coiffed, complemented by barely there wrinkles that made him look really smart and rich.

He offered his hand and lifted me off the floor.

Then, as most New Yorkers do after stumbling upon an emergency and realizing there is no dead body, the gawkers went about their lives like nothing had happened. The escalator turned on, and just like that, I was nothing more than an annoyance, blocking the way.

The man gently pulled me aside. "You okay?" he asked, his voice sending goosebumps up my spine.

I looked down at my now-frayed skirt, then back at the man. "Yes, thank you."

"No problem," he said with a wink.

I felt a spark of electricity between us, but then told myself I was imagining it. A man like him would never go for me.

"My name is Jack Holden. Yours?"

Butterflies.

"Betty Lou Abbott—Betts. They call me Betts."

His smile widened. "Lovely to meet you, Betts Abbott."

Just then, someone called out, "Dr. Holden! You're needed onstage for your speech."

A pair of middle-aged women wearing matching name tags that read STAFF approach us.

"I've got to run," he said, winking again. "It was wonderful to meet you, Betts. Steer clear of the escalators next time."

As the women pulled him away, Dr. Jack Holden did what every woman dreams about, reenacting the quintessential heart-melting scene in every romantic movie. He looked over his shoulder, found me through the crowd, and smiled.

And that's the story. That's how I met Jack.

We married a year later.

Six months after that, Jack retired, and together we packed up our (his) New York apartment and moved across country to his hometown of Weeping Pines. I didn't even think twice about leaving my job, my life in New York. In Weeping Pines, I accepted a position as the school counselor and settled into what would surely be my happily ever after.

If I'd only known then how wrong I was.

12

BETTS

Present day

Sex with Ian is cold. No emotion whatsoever. Mechanical, like two puppets with rusted joints awkwardly rubbing against each other. You come, I come. Done.

Afterward, Ian wipes himself down, tosses the towel in the corner, and picks up his phone. I pick up mine, and we retreat to our opposite sides of the house.

Something is going on. I am sure of it.

Don't get me wrong, I've been bored with our sex life for the last twelve months. But *he* seemed to enjoy it. Ian took pride in pleasing me, would whisper dirty things in my ear, sometimes even a grand declaration of love.

He was totally oblivious to the fact that I faked at least one in three orgasms, and when I did come, it was only because I imagined other men while he was on top of me. Usually movie stars, and sometimes random people from Weeping Pines. Sometimes the homeless man who sleeps behind the gas station downtown. Not sure why.

But tonight was different. There was no moaning, no sweet nothings, no pride in pleasing me. He avoided eye contact, burying his nose in my neck. It also took him longer to come than usual, his dick only halfway hard when he finally orgasmed.

And so it begins, I think. That phase in a relationship when a man becomes bored of the pussy he's laid claim to. His animalistic instinct kicks in, and he must find another pussy to make him feel like a king. A younger, tighter pussy. Always different from the one he already has.

And so, *I* begin.

The first thing I do is begin paying attention to my fiancé's phone activity.

Sure enough, all the signs are there. Ian rarely allows his phone out of his sight, carrying it with him everywhere he goes, even while at home. To the bathroom, to the den, to the refrigerator, it is always in his pocket or in his hand. Or facedown, so I can't see when a message pops onto the screen.

But then I notice that, in the evenings, he initiates the Do Not Disturb function. That little half-moon symbol that shows up in the upper right corner of the phone when the owner doesn't want notifications to display. In other words —when they don't want their wife to see their mistress messaging or calling them, regardless if the phone is face up or facedown.

I wait until he falls asleep on the recliner to make my big move. Using his face to unlock the phone, I click into his messages. Nothing suspicious. I go through his apps, also nothing suspicious. I make a note to search the den for a burner phone later.

Before replacing the phone on the end table, I add my fingerprint to the Touch ID, so no matter how many times

Ian changes his password, I will always have access to his phone. Then I install a secret tracking app, linked to my phone.

I become fully immersed in my new quest, my purpose in life.

Catching my cheating lover.

After all, I have been here before.

13

NICHOLAS

*B*etty Lou Abbott was diagnosed with antisocial personality disorder at age fifteen.

Before receiving the official diagnosis, she was diagnosed with anxiety, ADHD, depression, bulimia, and full possession by Satan himself. She spent most of her childhood in and out of medical clinics, therapy centers, hospitals, and rehabilitation facilities until her parents finally gave up. Tens of thousands of dollars spent on a girl who simply just didn't care.

Her parents, Carl and Ellen, divorced when Betty Lou was fifteen, a marriage lost to the constant attention demanded of a mentally ill child. Their only child.

There are many rumors surrounding Betty Lou and her family, the most entertaining involving voodoo and witchcraft. The rumors are bullshit, however, because Betty Lou is not nearly as unstable as everyone would like to think her to be.

Despite sharing the same disorder as Ted Bundy, the Son of Sam, and at least a dozen other of the world's most notorious serial killers, Betty Lou was—and is—a fully functioning, highly intelligent woman. She is witty, charming, and fun to be around.

She just doesn't give a shit. Not only about rules, boundaries, or fitting into social norms, but also about hurting other people's feelings. Children, teens, adults, no one is safe from Betty Lou's lack of empathy.

I've studied this phenomenon ad nauseam—well, since Betty Lou entered Jack's life, anyway. There are many theories about the physiological effects of this disorder, but in layman's terms, it's literally like she is lacking the part of the brain that feels for other people.

Betty Lou is selfish, uncaring, and self-absorbed, but not in a cocky way. In a tunnel-visioned kind of way. If anything, I believe Betty Lou to be extremely insecure. She is also extremely manipulative.

In the fourth grade, Betty Lou joined the Ozark Club for Girls. Kind of like Girl Scouts but without all the politics and sexual assault. This was urged by her mother in an effort to expand her daughter's social/emotional capacity.

During their annual bake-a-thon, Betty Lou decided she was going to win the badge for the most money raised that year. And with no regard to consequence, she set out to do just that, sabotaging her team's cookies by secretly replacing the sugar with salt, and thereby rendering six dozen cookies inedible.

Betty Lou then stole money from her mother's purse, rode her bike to the local discount grocery store, where she purchased ten boxes of off-brand cookies. She repackaged them as homemade, marketed them as vegan and gluten-free (they weren't), and charged double the price. For the cherry on top, she blamed everything on her "best friend." Betty Lou was kicked out of the club, and her reputation as, well, unstable, was solidified.

This story fascinated me. At only ten years old, Betty Lou cared so little about getting caught and losing friends that she didn't even bother to cover her tracks. She only wanted to win. Nothing else mattered.

The lies and manipulation grew in severity as she got older.

At fifteen, Betty Lou convinced her classmate to skip school, steal her father's new truck, and spend the day dirt-roading. The truck got stuck in a river, and eventually got flooded. Betty Lou offered to hike to the nearest road to flag down help while her classmate waited with the truck—except Betty Lou didn't call for help.

Instead, she hitchhiked home, where she ate dinner with her family and went to bed while her "friend" spent a frigid and terrifying night trapped in the middle of the woods. When the girl didn't come home from school, her parents called the police and initiated a search party. For nine hours, the girl's parents thought their daughter had been kidnapped. All while Betty Lou slept in her bed.

By age seventeen, Betty Lou was on enough medication to sedate a silverback gorilla. Prozac, carbamazepine, lithium, sleeping pills as needed.

For the next handful of years, Betty Lou appeared to get her act together. She graduated from high school and got accepted into community college, where she studied psychology. I, to this day, believe Betty Lou chose this field of study for no other reason than to serve as the biggest fuck-you to her parents and every one of the doctors who wrongly diagnosed and medicated her.

After receiving her bachelor's degree, Betty Lou fraudulently obtained her certificate to practice counseling.

Betty Lou is not a doctor.

The diplomas in her basement "office" are forged. The

accolades, the articles she supposedly authored, the studies attached to her name, are fake.

Fake, fake, fake.

I could arrest her on this alone. The fact that she is treating patients illegally would just be the icing on the cake.

But Betty Lou's ridiculous secret life is the last thing I care about. You see, I believe Betty Lou Abbott (who never took Jack's last name. Why? How weird is that?) edited his will.

Edited *me* out.

I want to be clear here: this isn't about the money. It's about how the man who so selflessly took me under his wing—fed me, mentored me, donated both his time and money to invest in me, a poverty-stricken, aimless teenager —was conned by a manipulative sociopath.

I'd like to say I don't understand why Jack fell in love with Betty Lou. But that would be a lie. She is beautiful, smart, charismatic. Unfortunately, she is also bat-shit crazy.

Jack was fooled. Conned. And the day he died, I made a vow to right this wrong.

The hours I have spent researching Betty Lou Abbott are exhaustive. The friends and family I've spoken to are countless, each happier than the next to share stories about the girl who wronged them in so many ways.

I have become obsessed. Yes, I wholeheartedly admit this. Through this journey, I, myself, have forged a path riddled with lies and manipulation.

And tonight's activities are no different.

Dusk settles on the horizon in a long orange line as I turn off the engine. The small town of Weeping Pines twinkles below me. I roll down the windows and inhale the cool autumn air.

In the rearview mirror two yellow headlights cut through the trees.

A black Tahoe rolls to a stop next to mine, the lights click off.

I shift in my seat, feeling a sudden spark of energy, like I have just taken a shot of espresso.

She does this to me.

The passenger door opens. Carmen slides onto the leather seat and quietly shuts the door. She is wearing all black. A black skirt, and a black leather jacket over a black cashmere sweater. It is my favorite color on her.

She knows this. She exploits this.

The glow of the radio illuminates her smooth tanned skin as she smiles at me.

"Hey there, handsome." The smile quickly turns into a frown. "You look tired. What's wrong?"

Carmen's candor is one of the things I love most about her—she is blunt and to the point. Black and white. There is no gray area. I never have to wonder what she's thinking. If she's happy, she tells me. If she's sad, she tells me. If she's mad, she hits me.

I run a hand over the top of my head, a habit I've had since childhood when I don't want to talk about something.

"What's wrong," she asks again, pressing.

"I spent the day at a brutal crime scene."

Her almond-shaped eyes widen. "At Edith's scene?"

"No. Different one. A murder/suicide."

"Oh, I heard about it. I'm so sorry. I heard it was really messy."

The word messy doesn't cover it. A sixteen-year-old boy broke into an elderly woman's home and stabbed her to death—thirty-six times, to be exact. Then he stuck the barrel of a shotgun in his mouth and pulled the trigger. Half his brain was stuck to the living room wall, the floor pooled with the elderly woman's blood.

"Is that why you're here?" Carmen asks.

I nod.

"Here" is a place of refuge. A location in the middle of a nature preserve just outside of town. It's a spot I found when I worked as the game warden, before becoming the county detective. It's a small clearing off an old logging road that no one uses anymore. Shaded by pines so tall they look like they touch the sky, the spot overlooks the town. *My town.*

Carmen puts her hand on mine. "I'm sorry, and I'm sorry about Edith."

"Why?"

"She was your nanny for, what, six years?"

"Seven." I don't want to talk about it, so I nod to the paper bag in Carmen's other hand. "Whatcha got?"

She lifts the sack. "Dinner."

My brows arch.

She smiles, leans in, kisses me on the cheek.

I turn fully toward her, gently grab her chin. My thumb trails her bottom lip. A moment passes as we stare at each other.

"In that case," I say, "I'm glad I did this."

Carmen gasps as I retrieve a single rose from the pocket of my door. "Where did you—is this for me?"

Her reaction pleases me more than I expected. For a moment, I feel like a child, giddy with excitement and validation.

I don't like it.

"I love it." She gushes, makes a show of sniffing the velvety black petals. "I'm going to post it the second I get home."

I say nothing, even though I don't like how much

Carmen posts on social media, how cavalier she is about sharing her life with strangers.

She contemplates the paper bag and frowns. "Now I feel bad about the ham-and-cheese melt. Should've sprung for the steak."

I grab her wrist and pull her to me. "I don't care about the food."

"No?" Her eyes flicker with heat. She scoots closer.

"No. I want you. Now."

Carmen grips the collar of my shirt and swings her leg over my lap as I push back the seat. Her skirt slides up around her waist.

She pins me in place. "We have things to discuss, Detective."

"Later," I mutter.

"Later? Yeah?"

"Yeah." I wrap my hands around her waist.

I need this. *Her.*

"When?" she asks.

"Later."

"Nicholas, you promised—"

"Later."

"Okay, boss," she teases before colliding with my lips.

My body surges to life, pinpricks spreading over my skin like fire.

Life. This is what she does to me. Makes me feel alive. She is magic, this Carmen. And if I am not careful, I will become addicted. I am too close already.

I slide my fingers between her legs, pull aside her lace panties.

She unzips my fly, unfolds my erection. There is no foreplay. There never is with us.

She spreads her knees and lowers on top of me, and

with one slow roll of her hips, she wipes it all away. The stress of the day, the tight muscles, the racing thoughts. Gone. Just like that.

Nothing else exists in my world at that moment. No thoughts, no deadlines, no reminders tapping on the fringes of my memory.

Nothing.

It is all her, that scent of cherry, that tight warm vise sheathed around me.

I am consumed. I want to crawl inside her and never leave.

I grab her hips, thrusting upward. We move together like animals, wild, unbridled, driven by the carnal need for sex.

The truck shakes. Sweat beads on our skin.

I wrap my fingers around her neck, pressing the pad of my thumb into the shallow pool of skin at the base of her jugular.

Her nails dig into my shoulders.

I squeeze harder, moaning her name as she gasps for air.

We come together.

Tears fill my eyes.

14

I wrote all night long. The words poured out of me, the sci-fi/young-adult something revealing itself faster than I could write.

I read a quote once that said, "You don't write the story; the story writes you." This was like that. It was like a switch flipped inside me, and someone else was speaking through me. I can't remember the last time I felt this kind of excitement.

It felt good.

Right.

The next morning, I wake up with a raging hangover. I am cold, but sweating, and based on my reflection in the nearby window, I am also deathly pale. This makes me immediately think of my fiancé. I look over. He is not next to me.

I look at the clock.

Shit.

I sit up and grab my head, my blood pulsing like a jackhammer at the temples. I've slept until nine-thirty in the morning. How can this be? I haven't slept past seven a.m. since college.

Doctors never sleep in.

I sit there a moment, waiting for the nausea to subside as I listen to the house around me. Is Ian home? No, he should be at work. Why didn't he wake me?

I drag myself out of bed. The moment I stand, my stomach rolls. I sit back down and take a few deep breaths. Slowly, the haze in my head begins to clear, and I remember the dirty little things I did the night before. Most notably, installing a tracking app on my cheating (I think) fiancé's phone.

Suddenly, the morning begins to look up.

I stumble my way down to the kitchen. The scent of toast lingers in the air. Ian has only recently left for work. I'm angry that he didn't wake me.

As the coffee brews, I review my appointment calendar for the day. At ten o'clock—in thirty minutes—I have a meeting with Tyler and Becca Hoover. Tyler is a teenage boy who was caught abusing the family dog in secret. Becca, his mother, owner of the only accounting firm in town, does not want to risk exposing this extremely disturbing behavior, for obvious reasons, and therefore has sought my discreet services.

From my reading, I know that animal abuse is the most common precursor to a slew of violent disorders. Because of that, I also know that, at this point, the responsible thing to do would be to refer Becca and her son to an *actual* clinic, so that the boy's violent tendencies would be legally recorded and on record.

Maybe next time. Tyler has only recently started opening up to me. And also, I am completely enthralled with this interesting young boy, and have a bet with myself on when he will finally cross the line and kill the dog.

After that appointment, I have blocked off two hours, from eleven to one, to work on my manuscript.

I shower, dress, pull myself together, and step into the basement just as Tyler's mom parks behind the house. I'll have to familiarize myself with the tracking app I installed on Ian's phone later.

I settle in, fold my hands on the desk, and take a deep breath.

Showtime.

By lunchtime, the sweats have subsided but the headache remains. I mix a cocktail, half Sprite, half vodka, and after teaching myself how to navigate the tracking app —it's ridiculously easy—and confirming Ian is at work, I fall asleep on the couch, my unfinished manuscript on the floor next to me.

I wake up to the sound of footsteps and voices in the room above me. Laughter—a *woman's* laugh. I sit up, my mouth feeling like cotton, my brain fuzzy.

It is three o'clock in the afternoon.

I push off the couch, smooth my hair. I'm still wearing the semi-professional blouse and jeans from my morning appointment, but now the shirt is badly wrinkled. I don't care because my attention is laser-focused on who the hell is in my house.

I emerge from the basement to find my fiancé and Carmen Marquis chatting in the kitchen. She is a vision of boho chic in a fitted black sweater tucked into flared jeans.

Ian is wearing a suit jacket over his usual uniform of dress shirt and slacks.

He *never* wears a suit jacket.

Wearing bright, wide smiles, they turn as I enter the room.

"Well, hey there," I say.

"My God, I love your house," Carmen says.

"Thank you." I shoot a look at Ian.

"Carmen was pulling up just as I got home," he says quickly. "She mentioned she's never seen inside the main house before, so I invited her in."

"I had a few minutes before our appointment," Carmen adds breezily.

"An appointment?"

"Yes." She frowns. "At three o'clock."

"Today?" The calendar above the coffeepot has nothing written in the afternoon box. "Are you sure?"

"Yes. I mean . . . yeah, I'm pretty sure."

Ian has now busied himself with a bottle of water.

I glance again at the calendar. I never forget appointments. Late, yes, but never forget them altogether. She's wrong. She has to be.

I think of the last time I checked her social media, an hour before I fell asleep. A zing of panic flies through me. What has she been doing? Where has she been? What have I missed? The problem with napping is that the world continues to turn while you are passed out.

"Okay, well, my mistake then," I say. "You can go downstairs if you'd like—down the hall, second door on the left. Give me a second and I'll be right down."

"We can reschedule if—"

"No. No, it's fine. Like I said, my mistake."

"Sure, okay."

My eyes never leave Ian as Carmen breezes out of the kitchen. I wait to speak until I hear the basement door close.

"I don't appreciate you inviting my clients into the house. My office is in the basement for a reason."

Ian sets down his water bottle. "Sorry. She asked if she could see around, and I said sure. It isn't a big deal."

"It is a big deal. I don't like—"

Ian cuts me off with a groan. "*God*, Betts, don't do this." He drags his fingers through his hair and begins pacing.

"Do what?"

"This." He gestures dramatically between us.

"*What?*" I mock his gesture.

"Start a fight. Be weird. Possessive of me."

"Get over yourself, Ian. It's not about you. I don't like random people in our house. I also don't like that you always forget to lock the doors, and I really don't like that my grandmother's diamond earrings were stolen the week after you moved in because of it."

"Jesus *Christ,* Betts, no one broke into the house and stole those damned earrings. It is not my fault."

"You *never* lock the doors. Ever."

"No one broke in!"

"So, I'm crazy and misplaced them, is that what you're saying?"

"No—I just . . ." He shakes his head as if there's no more energy left in him.

"Please remember to lock the doors and be prudent of allowing people in. It's not like we have a ton of extra money lying around to replace things that go missing."

He slowly turns toward me, like a doll on a spindle, his mouth agape. "I am *so* sick of you holding that loan over my head."

Then go get a better job and pay it back.

I don't say it. I don't need to. Ian receives the message loud and clear. His shoulders slump and he slinks out of the room like a whipped dog.

That's right, I mentally say to his spineless back. *No one as beautiful as Carmen Marquis would ever go for a bankrupt dentist. And don't ever forget it.*

I walk downstairs and make a show of slipping behind my desk, the power position of the room. Carmen has taken her usual seat on the client couch. I click through a few random files on my computer, pretending to refresh myself on our last meeting.

"So," I say, "what would you like to talk about today?"

"What would you like to talk about? You're the therapist."

"I'm curious why you came back to Weeping Pines six months ago."

"That's random. What makes you curious about that?"

"It feels like a big decision. You left Weeping Pines and moved to none other than Los Angeles, the place where dreams come true, yes?"

"So they say."

"Where you live for years, laying roots—one might say —and hit a few bestseller lists with your writing career. Then you just . . . disappear . . . only to remerge in this suffocating small town. Why? Why come back?"

"Why didn't you leave this suffocating small town after your husband died?"

"I like the house."

Carmen nods. "Okay, I get that."

"I also like my fiancé."

She doesn't take the bait.

"But you didn't inherit the grand, infamous Gadleigh Estate . . ."

"No, unfortunately you're correct."

"So, why? Why come back?"

"I had business to attend to."

"Business, huh?"

"That's right."

"Care to elaborate?"

"No."

"I don't believe you."

"That's your decision."

"I think you're running from something."

"There is a lot to run from in LA, I'll give you that."

"Not for someone like you, Carmen."

Interested, she tilts her head to the side.

"I think only two things would drive you away, or back home, I should say, to an area of comfort."

"Indulge me, Doctor."

"A man or a record."

"I'm assuming we're not talking about vinyl."

"Depends what you're into, I guess."

This time, she grins.

"So, which is it?" I ask. "A man, or did you get arrested for something? Or get caught up in something you couldn't sweet-talk your way out of?"

"Why not all three?" Her eyes twinkle. She's enjoying this little game as much as I do.

I lean back. "Okay, so you're not ready to talk about that yet. Soon?"

"Soon."

"Okay then, how's it going with hitting the deadline of your next book?"

"I'm almost back on track."

"You got your computer back?"

"Yes, thank God."

"Great. Glad to hear that. Are you getting enough sleep?"

"I'm working on it."

"Work harder. Sleep is important."

"Noted."

"And the woodpile? Have you had to use the axe again as an emotional outlet? Breaking things in a safe, controlled environment?"

"Not since I hurt myself."

"And how are your wrists?"

"Healed. Thanks for asking."

"Okay." I grab my pen and paper. "So, how many physical outbursts have you had since we last met?"

"Two."

"That's not bad. That's better, if I recall. Let's talk about them, is that okay?"

She nods.

I pretend to listen as, for twenty minutes, Carmen rattles off a ridiculous story about losing her temper.

Such a liar.

"So, for the next two weeks," I say, adding sparkles to the Christmas tree I've doodled on my notebook, "let's focus on destroying something smaller."

"Smaller?"

"That's right. We will go smaller, and smaller, and smaller, and in the process, you will begin to feel less and less satisfaction from the release, because, quite literally, a small object doesn't offer much of an explosion. And in doing so, the goal is that you release your need to break things altogether."

"What do you suggest I break this week?"

"Anything smaller than a log. I don't know, try an egg or something."

"I can do that."

"Good." The clock says we still have twenty minutes left in our session. "Would you like an *official* tour of the place?"

She perks up. "Yes, I would love that. Thank you."

I take Carmen through the mansion, room by room, making a point to linger in the den where Ian is sipping a beer, watching television. He ignores us.

I offer her a drink. She declines, disappointing me.

At four o'clock, I walk Carmen to her SUV. We book another appointment, say our good-byes.

As she opens the driver's-side door, my eyes widen on the object lying across the passenger seat.

A single black rose.

Exactly like the one that was placed on my late husband's grave days earlier.

15

BETTS

*J*an is late. He is never this late.

After Carmen left, he went back to the office to, quote, *catch up on paperwork*. It is now eight o'clock. I have been watching the driveway since he left.

I am debating on another glass of wine when a sudden wave of nausea rolls through my body, like the floor was suddenly pulled out from under me and I am falling at warp speed. This sickening feeling is immediately followed by a hot flash.

I bring my fingertips to my forehead and close my eyes in a feeble attempt to gather myself.

No luck.

How much have I had to drink?

I grab the window frame, slide my glass on the sill.

Another wave of nausea comes, followed by a spearing headache. Bile rises up my throat. I spin around and stumble toward the kitchen sink, but my stomach begins seizing with violent cramps, so I pivot and dart to the bathroom next to the laundry room.

I barely make it in time.

Thirty minutes, I sit on the toilet, wishing myself dead. When I am finally able to stand, I am soaked in sweat and as pale as a ghost.

I retrace my steps, wondering what brought on such violent sickness.

I study the bottle of wine I drank from. Nothing appears odd about it, but I throw it out anyway. I check the glass—did I forget to clean it? Maybe something moldy had slipped inside?

I take mental inventory of everything I'd eaten that day. My last meal was a small bowl of granola with fresh blueberries.

Frowning, I pull open the refrigerator door and stare at the small bowl of berries I keep in the fridge. I pull them out and study them.

I'm sure I washed and dried them after purchasing them from the farmer's market last weekend. Right?

Maybe I didn't.

My eyes narrow.

I recall the appointment Carmen and I had days earlier where she mentioned the woman who tried to poison her husband with nightshade, a toxic berry that resembles blueberries.

As I'm emptying the remainder of the blueberries into the trash can, I glimpse outside the kitchen window. I imagine the dark figure I saw—or that I think I saw—watching me from the trees.

I picture Carmen's face.

I picture Ian's face.

I turn from the window, glancing above the refrigerator where I keep a gun hidden.

Someone knows.

16

BETTS

I wake to my doorbell ringing. Since when did my house become the neighborhood Starbucks?

I roll over—Ian is not here, of course—and look at the clock. Eight-thirty a.m. He must be at work.

I consider ignoring the bell, but after a blast of knocks follows, I get up. As I throw on my robe and wiggle into my slippers, I notice a small plastic cup of pills next to a glass of water on the nightstand.

Ian.

I study each one, and once I feel confident that they are my correct prescription pills, I knock them back. But instead of picking up the water, I grab the half-empty bottle of wine sitting on the dresser. I take a few chugs and then shake my head and shoulders like a dog coming in from the rain.

I am half hoping that whoever is at my door has given up as I take my time walking through the house.

I'm not that lucky. Detective Stahl stands on the other side of the front door.

Stahl is an attractive man, there is no question about it. In fact, not long after Jack died, I considered making this known. This morning, however, there is something different about him that I can't quite put my finger on. He is freshly showered and shaven and dressed in a suit. Alert, with the kind of look in his eye that makes you snap to attention.

He smiles, a sparkle in those dark irises. "Did I wake you?"

"No."

He glances down at my robe, my slippers, then back up to my puffy eyes, which surely have little crusties in the corners. "I passed Ian on the way over."

"Cool."

He glances over my shoulder. "Is that coffee I smell?"

"No, I was actually just about to make a pot."

"Fantastic. I could really use a top-off." He lifts the large silver travel mug in his hand that I hadn't noticed. Sneaky bastard.

"Well, how ironic," I mutter. "Come on in, then."

I step back, making a note to install the outside security cameras I've been bugging Ian about. How wonderful would it have been for him to see this visit from Nicholas. The second in just a few days. What a lucky girl I am.

Stahl steps over the threshold, his ever-present scrutiny sweeping the house.

I shut the door.

The detective follows me to the kitchen and pauses by the window as I beeline it to the coffeepot.

"Supposed to be beautiful weather today."

"Is it?" I scoop grains into the filter, spilling half onto the counter.

"Yep. The tourists are starting to come in droves to see the leaves. The Pinetree Motel is already booked solid for two weeks."

I decide then that I want him gone. Immediately.

But Stahl continues in a breezy tone like we are old friends, just catching up. "Oh, and Jim at the Diner? You know Jim, right? Said he had a line out the front door until closing time yesterday. Had to keep Tammy—that new waitress he just hired—two extra hours just to clean up."

I have no idea how many scoops I have added to the filter. I can *feel* him watching me.

"Seems like the town is picking up for the next few months," he says with a stretch. "That'll be nice. We need the revenue. Speaking of, how's Ian's business doing?"

"Ian's business?"

I press the brew button. Is this about Ian's dentistry? Has he committed tax fraud when I wasn't looking?

I turn and lean against the counter as the coffeepot spits to life. "Well, thanks to Sparkling Smiles, I think he's having trouble keeping up with the regional chains."

"Damned big-box stores come in and take all the money away from our small businesses."

A second of dead air passes between us.

"Yep," he says. "Tough times for some folks. This whole Covid thing has got the world knocked off its axis. I know the government was offering loans for people with small businesses. Hopefully, Ian got in on that."

"If you have questions about Ian's business, I can call him. Or you can go to his clinic. I don't think he really picks up until after nine o'clock."

If "picking up" means surfing porn sites in his office.

"Oh no, no. I'm just making small talk. Forgive me. I know the fact that his business isn't doing well is probably kind of hard on you guys. Lots of marriages are falling apart these days."

"We're not married."

"Ah, that's right."

I top off the detective's travel mug and return to my side of the kitchen, where I pour my own coffee. I lean against the counter and cross my legs at the ankles. I take a long sip, eyeing him over the rim.

"But," Stahl says, "I'm sure you and Ian don't have that problem. You've been together for what? Two years now?

"About that."

Stahl nods, then takes a sip. "You know, I was talking to Jenny at the Diner yesterday. She mentioned that you and Ian knew each other long before you got engaged." He pauses, holding my gaze for a minute. "You know, while you and Jack were married."

"Is that so?"

"Yep. Said she saw you two having lunch at the city park once. Let's see, when was that . . ." He looks up, scratching his chin. "Oh—she said it was in the spring. Enjoying the budding leaves, she guessed. Let's see . . . that would have been several months before Jack died of a heart attack."

My body stills.

Stahl waves a dismissive hand in the air. "You know what a gossip she is, though. I don't believe a word she says. Even when she said she'd heard that your marriage was on the rocks right before Jack died."

My fingertips tighten around the mug.

Stahl laughs. "I told her she's been watching too many crime shows. But she pressed, suggesting you and Ian were having an affair. She said, verbatim, 'He's in a bit of a financial pickle with his company, and oh, look at that. Jack suddenly dies, and she gets more than a million dollars in life insurance.'"

"Jenny has quite the imagination."

"That she does."

Our eyes meet. Linger.

"You know Jack had a long history of heart problems," I say. "You know that better than anyone."

Stahl nods. "That he did. He certainly did." He looks out the window. When he turns back to me, he smiles. "Well, thanks for the top-off."

"If you're wanting to talk to Ian, you can catch him at his clinic."

"Thanks. I'm due for a cleaning. I might do just that." Stahl turns, but then pauses. "Oh. Almost forgot." He pulls a handful of mail from his suit pocket and hands it to me. "I got your mail for you. I'm sure it's annoying to walk to the end of that long driveway every day."

I grab the mail from him and toss it on the counter. "Thanks."

"No problem, and thanks again for the coffee."

I follow Stahl to the front door, watching as he starts his engine, then backs down the drive.

The second his truck disappears into the trees, I lunge to the railing and vomit.

17

BETTS

Four years earlier: Boston

$\mathcal{M}$iss Slutty Detective, I mused as I studied my alter ego in the mirror.

Under the brown trench coat cinched at my waist was nothing but scraps of lingerie attached to a lace garter belt and black hosiery. I'd shaved my legs, my armpits, and every single hair between my legs. I'd slathered myself in lotion, the really thick kind with the little gold sparkles that smells like a candy shop. I'd done myself up. Hot rollers, fake eyelashes, meticulously applied makeup, the works.

The convention was being held at a boutique hotel in Boston. Jack had been called to headline the event, sponsored by a pharmaceutical company who'd flown in doctors from all across the country. Their goal was to convince them to prescribe their next-gen migraine treatment, a bi-yearly IV infusion with little to no side effects (so they said).

My six-inch stiletto heels clicked loudly against the lobby floor, and it suddenly occurred to me that I could possibly be mistaken for a hooker.

I liked that feeling. I'd always admired prostitutes. Self-employed women who determine who, when, where, and how much, selling a product that will never—ever—go out of style. A product more addictive than cocaine.

Good for them.

It was my husband's fifty-first birthday. I'd given him the cake and gifts the day before he left. We'd FaceTimed that morning. I'd sung him happy birthday and tossed confetti in the air while managing to keep a straight face, knowing that his biggest gift was yet to come—*me.*

I'd arranged everything ahead of time. Spoken with the hotel manager, a portly woman with halitosis, who was more than eager to assist in my big birthday surprise. Together, we'd switched the credit card he had on file to mine, which was silly because our money came from the same place—his account. But still, it was a it's-the-thought-that-counts gesture.

After showing Halitosis my ID—to which she commented "beautiful"—I slipped the keycard to the presidential suite in my pocket.

"You'll have the champagne and cake sent up in an hour?"

"Yes," she said with a wink. "Exactly as you instructed."

"Thank you."

She glanced down at my trench coat and winked again. "Have fun."

I winked back and hurried to the elevator, careful to avoid the curious glances of the men. I did look good, and I appreciated the compliment of their stares, but I didn't want to be recognized. My husband was a bit of a celebrity in this arena.

I looked at my watch as the elevator zipped to the eleventh floor. It was five o'clock. I'd planned everything to the minute. My husband's last meeting had just wrapped up, and his group dinner didn't start until six thirty. He would be in his room, changing clothes and decompressing. (Jack was a bit of an introvert, despite his charming personality).

So, I had exactly ninety minutes to fuck my husband into oblivion, then send him dazed and satisfied to dinner, after which I would return home just in time to catch the ten o'clock news.

Bing, bang, done.

I caught myself grinning as I pressed the keycard against the lock and quietly pushed open the door. This whole alter-ego thing was exciting.

The suite was impressive, a multi-room parade of white leather, marble floors, and sweeping windows that overlooked the city.

No more than five steps inside, I caught a hint of vanilla in the air. My instincts piqued immediately.

A woman's perfume.

I will never forget that feeling for the rest of my life. My stomach dropped to my feet, a sickening mixture of dread and doom sweeping over me like a black cloud.

I knew instantly.

And the worst part? I'd never expected it. Not once. Never—*ever*—had I worried about infidelity in my brand-new marriage.

Adrenaline surged through my veins.

I stood there for a solid minute, frozen in inaction. And then I heard a moan.

A *woman's* moan.

There was no denying it now.

Jack is cheating on me.

I spun into action, grabbing a vase from the console table and propping open the door so that the sound of it clicking shut wouldn't announce my arrival. I slipped out of my heels, placing them neatly next to the vase. Then I tiptoed across the floor, my heart pounding.

Her moans became drowned out by his grunts. A sound I recognized immediately, the same ones he'd made on top of me so many times before.

I stepped into the doorway.

There he was, my husband, my Prince Charming, leaning back in a chair, his eyes closed, his arms folded behind his head. His pants were undone, his legs spread open wide.

A blond woman, completely naked, was on her knees in front of him. His dick was in her mouth, her head sliding back and forth as she gagged on his penis.

Awestruck, I stood completely frozen, watching my husband get sucked off until he came down her throat.

18

BETTS

Present day

*W*e all want simpler. It's in our DNA, at the very core of our genetic makeup. It's a survival mechanism. The wheel was invented to make life easier. The washing machine. Gunpowder.

We are built to solve problems. Recognize them, resolve them, then move on to the next.

Because there is always "the next," isn't there?

I've become very good at creating solutions to common problems over the years. Let me be clear here, I am not bragging. In fact, I am quite ashamed of this accomplishment. I've become a pro at solving problems meant for *women* to solve.

You know, like taking scissors to those goddamned dress shirts that are too hard to iron and then blaming the washing machine for shredding them. (Seriously, what *is* that fabric?). And learning which casseroles keep the longest so that I can make one at noon, keep it in the warmer all day (using *all* that electricity), then open a bottle of wine and read the afternoon away. Or removing the dust from the window blinds by spraying an entire bottle of Windex on them, then sitting back and watching the dust simply drip off. (It works. Seriously.) And last, but not least, perfecting the fake orgasm.

Yes, these are the problems *women* are supposed to solve.

Think about it. Who invented the wheel? Man. Who invented electricity? Man. The telephone, the internet, the light bulb, birth control.

Man, man, man, *definitely* man.

I have concluded that "simpler" simply means, no man. Death to the husband and all things wifey.

I have become one of those women who has slowly lost their light.

I want more. Is that so terrible?

Instead of battling depression, I, personally, am battling a disease called discontentment, though people will label it as something entirely different.

They are incorrect.

I was eight years old when I started wanting more. This was a side effect of growing up in the sticks of Arkansas, in a dilapidated house that was quite literally being held together by duct tape and staples. Sleeping through scorching summer nights without air-conditioning, and crowding against the warm refrigerator vent in the depths of winter. Wearing hand-me-down clothes purchased at rock-bottom prices from the mother of a popular girl in school who smoked Virginia Slims and used words like *phat* and *dope*.

Now, here I am at age thirty-nine, still feeling the same discontentment.

I watch from the window as my fiancé pulls up the driveway.

I take a deep breath, close my eyes, and exhale.

It's time for more.

~

"What the hell do you mean, Detective Stahl asked about my business?"

Ian drops his man-purse on the floor at the front door.

I hand him a glass of wine. I am wearing a proper 1950s housewife dress, high waisted, full bodice, crew neck. Very *I Love Lucy.*

"Yep," I say. "Came by this morning right after you left. Did he stop by your clinic?"

"This *morning*?" Ian stares at me, his eyes wide, an unattractive childlike expression on his face. "Why the hell didn't you call me?"

"It's not the first time the detective has stopped by, as you know."

"Yeah, but it's the first time he asked about *me*."

"Well, he said he was going to swing by your clinic. He didn't?"

"No, Betts, he didn't. What did he ask, exactly?"

"He asked how your business was going."

"What did you say?"

"Great."

"Good. What else did he ask?"

"If the business was in trouble."

"What? Why the hell would he ask that?"

"He asked if you're having financial problems, specifically."

"Financial problems? What a fucking son of a bitch." Ian shakes his head, processing, then stares at the wine in his hand for a minute. "I need to sit down."

As he breezes past me, I catch a floral scent. Like cherry blossoms.

Calm down, Betts.

Shut up, Betts.

I follow my fiancé into the kitchen. He sets the wine on the counter, displeased with the option I chose for him, and pulls a beer from the fridge. This makes me madder than the perfume.

Shut up, Betts.

I regard him closely as he sinks into the kitchen chair, pops the top, and takes a deep chug.

"I made a cauliflower-bacon casserole—low carb and keto—for dinner tonight."

Frowning, Ian says, "I need you to tell me exactly what happened."

"About the dinner or Stahl?"

Ian gives me a deadpan look.

"Well . . ." I lean against the counter, taking the weight off my aching feet. Damn the new heels. "Like I already said, he asked about your business, how it was doing, and if it was in trouble financially."

"I don't understand. Why would he ask that?"

"I don't know. You tell me."

Another deadpan. "You know the clinic's issues, Betts. There's nothing else aside from that."

Aside from the fact that it is turning zero profit? How about the money he owes me?

"Then he rather casually mentioned that he'd heard that you and I had become very close—his words exactly—in the months leading up to Jack's death."

I watch my fiancé very closely now.

A solid minute goes by as we stare at each other, the house so quiet you could hear a pin drop.

The *thing*.

Ian closes his eyes, takes a deep—albeit dramatic—inhale and then refocuses on me. "You mean to tell me Detective Stahl dropped by to ask about my business, implying that he is well aware of its financial issues, and then just so happens to add that you and I knew each other before Jack died—implying we were having an affair."

"I never said anything about an affair."

"Well, it sounds like that's what *he* was implying, doesn't it?"

"Sounds like he was implying much more than that." I sip my wine, watching Ian over the rim.

"And then what?" His tone has changed, a whisper of worry.

"Then I gave him coffee and sent him on his way."

My fiancé sits back, his brow furrowed in concentration.

I mentally catalog the way his breath has picked up, the tension in his shoulders, the twitch of his jaw. The way one eye is squinted just a bit more than the other, the telltale sign when he's thinking really, really hard. I can practically see the wheels turning in his head.

His eyes meet mine. "What aren't you telling me, Betts?"

My brows arch.

"No," he says as he shakes his head. "Don't do that. I don't want to play this game. What aren't you telling me? This is too weird."

"Let's start with you, Ian. Is there anything *you're* not telling *me*?"

He surges to his feet, sending the chair teetering backward and falling to the floor. "What the fuck is that supposed to mean, Betts? Jesus *Christ*, I am so sick of this shit with you. Always having to figure you out. Always feel like you're watching me. How much have you had to drink today, huh?"

I say nothing.

He jerks his chin to the wine. "What number glass is that for you? Third, fourth? Count *all day*—I'm not just talking about this evening. Did you drink when you woke up?"

Shut up, Betts.

Shut. Up.

"Don't think I haven't noticed." He steps forward, puffing out his chest in an almost aggressive stance. "The last six months—hell, the last year—your drinking has gotten completely out of control. And I know you hide it from me, along with a shit-ton of other things."

His eyes narrow.

"I saw you crying, heard you crying in the basement last week. I know about the damned folder you keep all Jack's shit in, the one you keep hidden in the bookshelf. I know you still cry over him, Betts. I fucking know it."

Ian begins pacing.

"You've changed over the last two years, Betts. Almost instantly after we got engaged. If you didn't want to get engaged, you shouldn't have said yes. You've changed so much since that day."

I set down my wineglass, careful to keep a steady hand. "Have I? How about you, Ian? I'm not the only one who's changed around here."

"Bullshit! Don't turn this around on me like you always do. You don't even take your anxiety medication regularly. Sometimes—sometimes, Betts, I feel like there is a lot I don't know about you. Sometimes, I think—"

"Be careful, Ian."

Shut up.

"Or what?"

Shut up.

We stare at each other. Ian looms over me, his fists clenched, his chest heaving with adrenaline.

Hit me. Hit me hit me hit me.

"Goddammit, Betts." He tears away his gaze and spins around. "I need to go."

"Where?"

"Out of here. Out of this fucking house."

I follow him out of the kitchen. "Where are you going?"

He ignores me, practically running from me, his shoulders hunched as if creating an invisible shield against the monster behind him.

"Ian! Where the hell are you going? To her?"

He stops suddenly. Slowly, he turns, his expression as cold as ice. "What do you mean, *to her*?"

A grin slowly crosses my face as I stare back at him.

That's right, dear fiancé. I know.

He shakes his head. "You're fucking crazy, Betts."

"Oh, honey," I whisper to his back. "I'm nothing compared to her."

19

BETTS

Three and a half years earlier: Upper East Side, New York

went for months acting like I didn't know. Months of replaying the memory of watching my husband get sucked off in his hotel room. The memory of his infidelity.

I often wonder what would have happened if I had announced myself and made my presence known, instead of grabbing my heels and slinking out the door like a whipped dog. I imagine the look on his face if he had opened his eyes and seen me, seeing him.

Would it be shock? Sadness? Fear?

What about her? What would *she* have done when she realized I, *the wife*, was there? That she was caught? Would she have screamed? Run?

What would *I* have done?

In the days following the discovery that my husband was a cheating bastard, I became obsessed with uncovering who this mystery woman was. My visual of her was limited— long blond hair and a skinny backside complete with sharp scapulas and protruding ribs. I didn't even know how tall she was, considering she was on her knees when I saw her.

Nonetheless, I vowed to find this woman. The woman who could give better head than me.

I began my search by sneaking into my husband's office and turning it upside down. Looking for receipts, pictures, love notes, burner phones, condoms.

I found nothing.

I called the clinic where he'd worked for decades before retiring, delicately inquiring about a young blond employee, past or present. This was tricky to navigate, of course, but between this and scouring the staff page on the website, I was able to gather a list of names. I memorized each of the women's Internet footprint. Printed pictures, made folders. But in the end, there was no way to tell who—if it had been any of them at all—he was cheating with.

There were so many questions, aside from her name.

How long had the affair been going on? Was she the only one? Was it serious or only about sex—and why did *that* matter so much to me? Which would be worse? And had they actually had intercourse, or was the line of my husband's moral boundary oral sex only? What if she gave him an STD? Do I now have an STD?

Finally, and most importantly, what am I lacking? Why am I—and I alone—not good enough to be the only woman in my husband's life?

Everything changed between us.

Looking back, this was my fault. I wasn't nearly as good at concealing my emotions as I am now. I allowed the tension to settle inside the house, to stick to the walls, to the floor, to us. Everything around and between us grew cold. I analyzed every single word that came out of my husband's mouth, his tone, the way he moved when he said it. In my mind, every sentence had fifteen alternate meanings, and I would analyze each one as I lay down to sleep.

I quit sleeping, actually, always hypervigilant to catch him in the act. A late-night text or call, whatever.

I quit taking my pills. I'm not sure why. Jack, being a neurologist and therefore well-educated on my issues, kept a close eye on my medications. I had to be sneaky about it.

I began making plans, moving assets, researching lawyers. Educating myself on the intricacies of divorce. For example, I learned that there is something called "conflicting out," a situation where one spouse meets (in secret) with the best divorce attorney in the area for an initial consultation, thereby disallowing this attorney to represent the other spouse, as it would be considered a conflict of interest. Basically, it's important to be a step ahead and secure my access to the best legal counsel in the area.

My sense of urgency increased.

Severing the binds of marriage consumed me. I ignored all else, at home, at work. Every second that I wasn't working, I was huddled behind the computer researching, reading articles and blogs about how to overcome the hurdles associated with divorce.

Educating myself on all the different paths I could take to get out.

20

BETTS

Present day

Carmen canceled her appointment with me via voicemail on my office line. She has my personal cell phone number—I gave it to her once. I don't know why she didn't use it.

I call her back. No answer.

An hour later, I call again.

No answer.

I call my fiancé, whom I haven't seen or spoken to since he stormed out the night before.

No answer.

I call his clinic, am told Ian is in a "meeting" and advised to call back later.

I click into the tracking app I installed on his phone. An error message pops up, indicating no connection.

Shit. He either found the app and deleted it, or . . . there is no "or." He found the damned app.

Shit, shit, shit.

I call Carmen again, then Ian one more time.

No answer.

Both Carmen and my fiancé are MIA—and avoiding *me*.

Coincidence?

Absolutely not.

I spend the afternoon stewing. Bottle of wine in one hand, phone in the other, I sit on the picnic table in the woods and stare at the screen, willing either Carmen or Ian to call me back. At that point, I don't care which one.

Once the bottle is empty, I make my way into the house, where I proceed to drink an entire carafe of coffee and eat a six-pack of waffles—extra butter and extra syrup.

By four p.m., there is no question in my mind that Carmen and my fiancé are having an affair.

When he left the house, I assumed he went to his clinic and slept on the couch (he has done this before). But now I am convinced he drove straight to Carmen's and stayed with her. And now, I am on a mission to expose the truth.

The road to Carmen's house is narrow and winding, and I'm grateful I had the good sense to dull my buzz with caffeine and carbs before getting behind the wheel.

According to the old real estate listing, Carmen's house is described as "a quaint beachside cottage with clifftop views."

Sounds glamorous, right? Not quite. The home is 800 square feet of rotting wood and dirty windows. An old structure badly in need of renovation. And the cliff it sits on isn't so much of a cliff as a steep slope. There's even a footpath that leads down to the beach.

The views alone sell the place, no question about it, and I remember gawking at the price tag. The woman is probably sleeping in a bed of termites and mouse shit. She'll never get her money back on the place, ever.

Idiot.

As I top the "cliff," I run into a bit of a snag. Carmen's driveway is incredibly short, and due to the terrain, there is no place to park and watch. I did not think this through.

I slowly drive by. Her black Tahoe sits out front. Ian's Subaru is nowhere to be seen, but that doesn't mean it's not there. A faded tire path disappears around to the back of the house. A perfect spot to hide a vehicle—she's probably hidden many men's vehicles before.

I drive by two more times, assessing. Another option is that Ian parked at the boardwalk a mile south and walked to her house.

So, I check there.

No dice.

After driving by one more time, I head back into town and drive to Bailey Dentistry. By now, it's five o'clock, so I am not surprised to see that Ian's car is not there. But I wonder, was he ever there today? Did he have his assistant lie when I called earlier?

I call him again. No answer.

I call her again. No answer.

I snag a vacant spot in front of the local diner, aptly named "the Diner," which is busy with the five o'clock rush.

"Is Jenny available?" I ask after pushing my way through the crowd to the register.

The barely sixteen-year-old waitress looks up, a bit wild-eyed, frazzled by the sudden onslaught of customers. I wonder if it's her first day.

"Uh, who?" she says in a jarringly low voice that doesn't match her appearance.

"Jenny . . ." *Shit.* I don't know Jenny's last name.

"Oh, uh . . ." The girl takes the check from a large, burly man draped in flannel who has elbowed his way next to me. "Yeah, she's here. In the back, I think." She begins adding up the man's receipt. *Tap, tap, tap.* "That'll be twenty-two sixty-three, sir."

The man grunts, then pays in cash.

"Do you think you can go get her for me?"

The girl flicks me a glance, and I can't tell if she's annoyed with me or scared of me. "Yeah, sure." She spins on her Converses and leans into the window that leads to the kitchen. The black lines of a tramp stamp peek out from her waistband.

I decide then that I like her.

"Hey, Jenny," she calls, and there's a sense of urgency in her tone that embarrasses me. "Someone's here to see you!"

"Be right out!"

"Thanks." I move aside, step on someone's toes—*"Ouch!"* then, *"Excuse me!"*—and stumble away from the two lines converging into one. Those leaving and trying to pay their tabs, and those waiting on a table.

I am suddenly irritated. This surge of annoyance is directed immediately at Ian—where it should be. Why the hell did he do this to me? Doesn't he know you can't cheat in a small town and get away with it?

The door to the kitchen swings open. I almost don't recognize Jenny at first. After all, the last time I visited this diner was with Ian, more than a year ago.

Wearing a brown apron over a faded denim button-up and a pair of jeggings that are stretched so thin it's a wonder the seams haven't popped, the fifty-something is at least thirty pounds heavier than I remember. Jenny's shoulder-length hair has grayed and is thinning, which she has attempted to mask by applying way too much product, which makes her hair look like a helmet. She is no longer wearing glasses, which is a shame. She needs glasses to hide the bags and wrinkles around her eyes.

She smiles warmly when she sees me, setting the tone. "Hey, Betts, good to see you. Been a while."

Jenny's casual demeanor suggests one of two things. Either she doesn't remember her chat with Detective Stahl where she suggested my fiancé is broke (he is), and that he and I were having an affair while Jack and I were still married. Or two, she didn't say it in the first place, and Stahl was lying to me. Baiting me.

"What's going on?" she asks.

"I was hoping we could have a quick chat? Maybe . . ." Indicating that I want privacy I say, "Maybe outside?"

A line of concern creases her hairy brow.

"Sure, sure. Come on back through here." As I follow Jenny through the kitchen, she speaks over her shoulder. "I've got four tables right now, so I've only got a sec."

"That's fine." I ignore the curious glances from the twin cooks who, together, probably weigh over six hundred pounds.

Jenny pushes through the back door, and we step onto a tiny square of concrete flanked by overflowing dumpsters. Flies swarm the cool air above us.

"So, what's going on?" she asks, fisting her hands on her hips.

"I had an interesting conversation with Detective Stahl yesterday."

Jenny's face instantly hardens.

Ah yes, she remembers.

"He mentioned that you implied that Ian and I had a relationship while Jack and I were still married."

"What? Did he?"

"Yes."

"I don't know why he would say that."

"So, you didn't say it?"

"No, I—no, I didn't."

"Well, that's not what he said."

Her frown deepens. She stares at me like I have two heads.

"Did he come talk to you?" I ask.

"No."

"He didn't stop by the Diner to talk to you?"

"No, he didn't come here. We ran into each other in the grocery store."

This time, I frown. This isn't aligning with the story Stahl told me while standing in my kitchen. He told me he spoke to Jenny at the Diner. I'm sure of it.

"And what did you two talk about?"

Jenny and I are both entirely uncomfortable now.

"Well, he did ask about you, come to think of it. Asked how well I knew you, considering we were neighbors for a while before Bert and I moved back into town."

"And what did you say?"

"I told him about the time I brought you the pound cake, you know that welcome basket right after you and Jack moved in?"

The one I never thanked you for. Yes, I remember.

I nod.

"We talked about that for a minute, and then we talked about the weather, and that was that. Really, it was no big deal. Hell, I'd even forgotten about it."

I study her closely. "Well, I guess I'm wrong then."

Jenny doesn't smile. Instead, she gives me a concerned look confirming what everyone thinks—I'm the crazy girl in town.

"I would never say such a thing," she says. "Jack was a good man. I wouldn't tarnish his name."

"Again," I say with a nod, "my mistake."

I go to reach for the door, but Jenny beats me to it and gestures me inside.

I feel the heat rising up my neck as we walk through the kitchen. Feel the release as I sweep my arm across the counter, sending no fewer than a dozen plates of food shattering on the floor.

21

NICHOLAS

"*D*o you miss it?" I ask.

"Miss what?"

"Writing. LA. Living in fantasyland."

"Sometimes."

I grab Carmen's hand and pull her toward me. "Don't step there."

"Why?"

"Blood."

She squints at the bloodstained rocks, then frowns. "I thought you said the police officially opened the scene this morning."

"They did, but that doesn't mean I'm done with it."

We consider the single-wide trailer ahead of us where two people were found dead days earlier. It is a sight in its own right, even without the stigma that will now follow wherever it goes.

Vertical slashes of rust and mildew streak the sides of the once-white aluminum siding. There are only two windows, both covered in strips of duct tape to prevent the cracks from spreading. A stack of cement blocks serves as the front stoop. Dead, moldy leaves cover everything—the ground, the roof, the broken-down truck that no one will ever drive again.

There is no yard, no landscaping. It is as if the trailer was simply dumped in the middle of the woods. A likely scenario, considering.

There is a stillness in the forest around us, a quiet that makes me itch. I'll never get used to it.

Carmen squats to study the bloodstained rocks. "They're drips of blood, not smears or transfers from boots."

"Correct."

"Why? How? How did the blood get outside?"

"She confronted him while he was trying to break in. This is where he first stabbed her. She didn't die quickly. She ran, tried to get away, and he just kept stabbing and stabbing her." I jerk my chin to the door. "Let's go inside first, then we'll walk the perimeter."

After a quick glance over my shoulder, I pull open the screen door, the rusty hinges squeaking loudly against the silence.

Carmen steps inside after me. "Oh my God," she mutters, covering her mouth with her hand.

A moment passes as we stand side by side, still and unspeaking, while she gathers herself.

I am used to the smell by now.

"I'm going to—"

"There is no throwing up here, Carmen. Pull it together."

She works a deep swallow, removes her hand from her mouth, and jerks her shoulders back. We are a united front. We must be. There is no room for weakness.

I'm not sure what Carmen is most disgusted with—the thick layer of newspaper and trash bags that cover the floor, the counters, and the chairs, every inch of it saturated with urine and feces from the forty-seven cats that were found eating the woman's dead body.

The cats are now being nursed back to health at the Weeping Pines animal shelter. The twelve dead ones we found in the closet were tossed in the trash can outside.

Or maybe it's the dried pools of blood that merge with the urine stains, or the single bloody fingerprint smeared on a window, as if someone were trying to pull themselves out in the seconds before death. Or perhaps it's the spray of dried blood, a massive splat of crimson dead center on the living room wall, and the chunks of skull, brain, and hair stuck to it.

I watch Carmen closely as she closes her eyes, taking a moment to compose herself, then turns to me.

She begins.

"Kit Elsher, white male, age sixteen. Resided with his mother—single mom, divorced, father currently resides in Mississippi—at 1214 Oak Road Lane, two blocks west of the town square. Average weight and height, size nine shoe. Unkempt, shaggy hair that he dyed black two years ago. Prefers dark clothing. Quiet, shy, a loner. Hobbies include computer games and listening to rock music. An outcast, according to his schoolmates. GPA of 3.1. Drives a 2001 Nissan, black.

"Victim two, Aurora Sanchez, Hispanic female, age seventy-one. A widow, husband died of prostate cancer four years ago. No criminal record, but the husband had two DWIs, a public intox, and spent a few months in the county jail for fighting. Ms. Sanchez is below average weight, suspected anorexia, with COPD from smoking. Her sole income is Social Security. Disorders include compulsive behavior, including hoarding and animal abuse. Suspected dementia.

"Elsher and Sanchez are not related, nor have any public connections to note. Scene suggests the kid stabbed the woman, then shot himself in the head. Police are operating under a murder/suicide assumption—however, there was no suicide note and nothing to immediately indicate the sixteen-year-old boy was contemplating suicide."

"Good job. Explain further."

"Elsher had recently applied to a local automotive training academy to become a mechanic. Also, he had a date with a girl in his class scheduled for the Friday night after he and Ms. Sanchez were found. This is not the behavior of someone who is planning to kill themselves."

I nod, and Carmen continues.

"Lastly, the angle at which he shot himself in the head doesn't fit the suicide story."

"Why?"

"Kit was left-handed. According to the gunpowder residue on his hands, he used his right hand to shoot himself. But he didn't . . . because he was left-handed. Also, there is no motive. The story being told is that Kit just randomly found the trailer in the middle of the woods and decided to stab an innocent woman to death. Things don't add up." Carmen looks at me. "Do the police know this?"

"That there are enough details to suggest that another player is missing from this game? That someone killed both Elsher and Sanchez and then staged it to be a murder/suicide?"

She nods.

I turn fully toward her, slowly run my thumb down her cheek. "Thing is, Carmen, people are stupid. They will always take the easy way out. They operate in their own interests, no matter what laws are broken or who they have to take down in the process."

"What are you going to do?"

"Let them sniff around a bit longer, then eventually point them in the right direction—which is Ms. Sanchez's cousin, Marco, who was recently released from prison and was seen selling drugs to Elsher the night of the murder. They'll link it. They need to learn on their own. They need to learn a lesson."

Carmen stares at me. Then—

"Nicholas . . ." She glances at the door. "I think Betts is starting to suspect something."

22

BETTS

Three and a half years earlier: Weeping Pines, WA

$\mathcal{I}$ didn't sleep my first night in Weeping Pines. I felt nervous and out of place. That sickening feeling that I wasn't where I was supposed to be. I was exhausted, both mentally and physically, but couldn't shut it off.

It had been a whirlwind few weeks.

One month earlier, my cheating husband had surprised both me and his colleagues with the news that he was going to retire, effective immediately. His colleagues suspected it had something to do with the announcement of the new young CEO, a forty-three-year-old Canadian neurologist.

My opinion? Jack's abrupt departure had absolutely nothing to do with the changing of the guard. I suspected it was something much more nefarious, such as an argument between him and one of his many mistresses. Perhaps a threat to expose their relationship, which would undoubtedly end the revered neurologist's career.

But retiring wasn't the only news he had. Jack also wanted to leave the city and move back to his hometown of

Weeping Pines, clear across the country. He wanted a slower pace of life, he'd said.

Okay, I'd said.

I packed up our penthouse suite and moved with my husband out of the Upper East Side to a tiny speck on the Washington coast.

Needless to say, this sudden change in plans put my divorce musings on hold. Leaving New York meant my husband leaving his mistresses. It meant that his focus would be back on me, his wife, where it should have been all along.

For a fleeting moment, I felt hopeful.

To say the move to Weeping Pines was a culture shock is an understatement. Not only in the change of pace and the type of people, but in Jack himself. He was a local hero, slipping seamlessly into the role of prodigal son returned. Everyone knew him—and no one knew me.

It didn't take long before the gossip mill started to churn. I was labeled a gold digger before I'd even taken my first trip to the grocery store.

Within weeks, Jack—and his infinite small-town power —secured me a job as student counselor at the Weeping Pines middle school, and just like that, that I had a completely new and different life.

I hated every fucking second of it. Then I had an epiphany.

My effort to get pregnant was twofold: One, fix things between Jack and me, and two, gain sympathy from the locals. Because who can hate a pregnant woman?

Eventually, I did get pregnant, but I had a miscarriage.

Three of them.

I began to resent Jack. Hell, I hated him. Not only because of the affair(s), but also because he'd dragged me to this boring small town that sits under a perpetual cloud of bleakness.

The days, the months, dragged on.

I hated my job.

I hated the teachers at the school.

I hated the kids.

Yet again, I began to contemplate divorce.

One night, drunk off wine, I sneaked into my husband's office and began snooping, eventually finding a leather-bound folder that held our most important documents— our financial information.

That night, I learned that my husband had $1.4 million in life insurance.

Five minutes later, I found myself sitting on my closet floor, laptop resting on my knees, researching the natural causes of death.

And the not-so-natural ones.

23

BETTS

Present day

*M*y phone vibrates on the picnic table next to me.

I set aside my notebook and pen and pick it up, hoping it is Ian. Almost two days, and I have heard nothing from my fiancé. I called his office first thing this morning, only to find out it was closed. Ian never closes his office during regular business hours.

I'm toeing the line between angry and worried. I considered setting up camp outside his office, but I've decided I have a bit too much pride for that.

At what point is someone considered a "missing person"?

Blowing out a breath, I pick up the phone. "Hello?"

"Hello, may I speak with Betty Lou Abbott, please."

"Speaking."

I turn away from the wind. It is late morning, dark and dreary. Thick gray clouds hang low in the sky, threatening rain. Fitting, I muse, for the current state of my mood.

"Ms. Abbott, this is Paul Whitehead from Pine Cemetery. I was just curious what you wanted us to do with the headstone."

I frown. "I'm sorry . . . what?"

"Your ex-husband's headstone. Jack. What do you want us to do with the headstone? Do you want us to deliver it to you, or—"

I blink, watching a bright orange leaf fall from the tree in front of me. "I'm sorry . . . who is this again?"

"Paul Whitehead from the cemetery."

"Okay. I—I'm not understanding. What's happening with Jack's headstone?"

There is a long pause on the other end.

"Well, ma'am, considering his body will no longer be here, I didn't know what you wanted us to do with it . . ."

"*What*?" I squeak. "What are you talking about?"

Another long pause.

"What's going on?" I am up on my feet now.

"Uh, well, it's my understanding that you wanted us to exhume your husband."

"*Exhume?*"

"Yes, that's correct. So, uh, yeah . . . do you want—"

"No. Do *not* exhume my husband. I do not want my husband dug up from the cemetery."

Paul drags in a deep breath. "Well, it's a little too late for that."

"What do you mean?"

"Well, ma'am, it's already done. Detective Stahl is here now, standing right next to me, ready to escort it—him—to the—"

"You said Detective Stahl?"

"Yes, ma'am."

"Don't move—don't do *anything* until I get there."

I disconnect the call, grab my notebook, and sprint to the house. I don't bother to change out of my dirty jeans and sweatshirt.

After pulling on a pair of boots, I grab my keys and jog out the door.

I turn my car—far too fast—into the cemetery entrance, fishtailing on the gravel. I glare at the silhouettes of two men standing next to a bulldozer in the corner of the lot. Another man, shovel in hand, waits idly nearby.

Heads turn as I slam on the brakes, my BMW skidding to a stop.

I get out, slam the door, and weave through the headstones, my eyes locked on Detective Stahl.

There is no smile today, no charm. His face is hard, his jaw tight, and I get the sense he is ready for a fight.

"What the hell are you doing?" I ask the second I am within yelling distance.

I see the dusty top of the casket, the one I picked out days after Jack's untimely passing. It sits next to a deep black hole in the earth where a massive worm wriggles around a severed root. My stomach churns.

"I just wanted to take another look at your husband's body," Stahl says. He meant it to sound casual—like, no big deal—yet his tone is anything but.

"Another *look* at his *body*?" I am unable to control my emotions any longer. This is a nightmare.

"That's right."

"So, you mean his *bones*?"

"Precisely."

"Why?"

"Well, in light of new information . . ."

"What new information?"

Paul, the cemetery groundskeeper, and his scrawny help take a collective step back, out of the line of fire.

I continue, uncaring of their presence. In fact, I think it's a good thing to have witnesses at the moment. "Are you referring to the fact that you think Ian and I were having an affair before Jack died?"

"That, among a few other things."

"Well, we weren't. And if you think Ian and I killed Jack so that we could get his insurance payout, only to turn around and use that money to fund Ian's stupid little dentistry, you're sorely mistaken. You are barking up the wrong tree, Stahl."

The detective tilts his head to the side. "Now, I never said any of that."

"Don't patronize me. You implied it. Listen, I know you and Jack were close, that he was like a father figure to you— I get it. But you have no right to do this . . . Wait a second. You *literally* have no right to do this. There's got to be a law against this. I was—*am*—Jack's sole beneficiary. I make all the decisions, and I didn't consent to this. I *don't* consent to this. Stop it right now, or I'm going to—"

"Too late for that."

"No, it's not!" I sound like a child. "Just lower it back down and cover it back up."

All three men stare at me like I am an idiot.

I jab my fingers through my hair as I begin pacing. "God, Detective, what the hell are you doing? You of all people know the laws here. You know I didn't consent to this."

"Ah, but you did."

I freeze, then turn slowly to him. "What the hell are you talking about?"

Stahl pulls a folded piece of white paper from his pocket.

I rip it from his hand, unfold it, and skim the letter that consents to exhumation of Jack Holden's body and additional forensic testing of the corpse—*and* to cremation afterward.

I gape at my signature, right there at the bottom, in bright blue ink.

I shake the letter at him. "I didn't sign this."

Stahl makes a show of peering down at the paper. "Looks like you did to me."

"This isn't my signature."

"Sure looks like it."

I shove the paper back at him. "I did *not* sign this."

The detective snatches the paper from my hand and closes the inches between us, his eyes as cold as ice.

A shiver runs up my spine.

"Ms. Abbott, is there a particular reason you do not want me to reexamine your husband's body so to confirm that nothing nefarious happened to him?"

My insides are literally vibrating with anger.

Stahl holds up his palms, as if to surrender, and takes a step back. Lowering his voice, he says, "But, you know, if you want to go call your lawyer, go for it. But you might want to cancel all those appointments at your *clinic* that you think no one realizes is operating illegally."

He looks up, scratches his chin.

"I wonder what the charges and fines would add up to if the Feds found out about it." He refocuses on me, his eyes narrowed. "And adding that to the incident at the Diner last night. Jim, the owner, a personal friend of mine, is ready to stick you with vandalism and disorderly conduct." He shrugs. "But I can advise otherwise . . ."

"You're an asshole."

I look down at the casket. I can't stomach it a minute longer. I feel like I am going to vomit.

"Would you like to stick around?" he asks, a curve now on his lips. "You can help."

Stahl already knows I'm going to allow him to continue this ridiculous charade. After all, he is right. I am operating an illegal clinic, and I did lose my shit at the diner. He is also correct that a grieving widow would—*should*—want to know if there is even the slightest hint that her husband's death was not innocent.

"No," I say as a wave of nausea washes over me. "I'm going to go."

"You need somebody to drive you home? You're a little green around the gills."

"Fuck you, Detective Stahl."

And with that, I turn, swallow the spit pooling in my cheeks, and make it to my car no fewer than two seconds before vomiting all over the tire.

24

BETTS

Three and a half years earlier

Strychnine is a chemical found in rat poisons. An odorless white powder that is extremely toxic if inhaled, taken by mouth, or mixed in a solution and ingested. Only a small amount is needed to produce severe effects, including death.

Almost immediately after ingestion, a person experiences painful muscle spasms, difficulty breathing, and eventually respiratory failure leading to death.

Strychnine is extremely easy to get. Shockingly so. Not only is it found on store shelves in the pesticide aisle, it is also found on the streets, commonly mixed with street drugs such as LSD, heroin, and cocaine.

In the event that strychnine is suspected in a fatality, a simple toxicology test is done during the autopsy to confirm or exclude this. However, an autopsy is *only* performed if specifically requested by either the authorities or the deceased's family.

25

BETTS

Present day

The figure is back.

Standing just inside the tree line, barely visible in the waning light. It is staring right at me, through the kitchen window.

This time, I am prepared.

I grab the pistol from the top of the refrigerator, cock it, and step outside. Wind whips through my hair, causing dead leaves to rain around me as I stride across the backyard, gun up, eyes locked on the unmoving figure.

I say nothing as I slide my finger over the trigger. I continue to advance, keeping the figure in my sights.

Still, the figure stands.

I pull the trigger.

The blow stops me, stunning me. The smell of gunpowder stings my nose as I open my eyes.

The figure is gone.

A fresh gash mars the trunk of the pine next to where the figure stood.

I stare into the woods, dark with shadows.
Next time, I think.
Next time.

26

BETTS

*I*t has officially been two days since Ian stormed out. Forty-eight hours since I have seen or heard from my fiancé. Forty-eight hours of me stewing in my own anger.

I canceled the three appointments I had scheduled. I am incapable of concentrating on anything else, let alone a dog-torturing teenager.

My thoughts have run all over the place, including wondering if Ian is in cahoots with Detective Stahl. Perhaps they don't hate each other, after all, and have bonded to conspire against me.

Was it Ian who forged my signature that allowed Jack's bones to be exhumed? This would make sense—he's certainly seen it enough to do so.

If not him, who?

I've called Carmen several more times—fine, nine, because ten would be just too much—under the guise of rescheduling the appointment she canceled days earlier.

No answer, no call back.

I've driven by her house six times—or is it seven now?—over the last two days.

Right now I am sitting in a leather chair in the reading room, staring out the window, watching the leaves fall one by one. I have been sitting here for hours.

I am drunk.

I am going mad.

I grab my phone and call Detective Stahl. He answers on the first ring.

"Hello, Stahl here."

"Detective. It's Betts."

"Ah, Betty Lou. Good to hear from you. I was a bit worried about you when you left the cemetery yesterday."

"Listen, this isn't about that. I . . . I'd like to know if you've seen my fiancé."

A long pause, then Stahl says, "Are you home right now?"

"Yes."

"I'm actually just a few minutes away. Mind if I drop in?"

I take a mental inventory of my appearance. I haven't showered, but did put on makeup, and I am wearing a cashmere sweater and black leggings. I look half decent.

"Sure," I say.

"I'll see you in a second."

Three minutes later, Stahl's truck rumbles up the driveway. I quickly finish dabbing gloss on my lips, then hurry out of the bathroom.

I wait until he knocks.

He smiles widely as I open the door. The charm is back. I appreciate the effort, and in all honesty, he is much more attractive when he smiles. I'm sure he knows this.

"Coffee?" I ask.

"Read my mind."

"I just put on a pot, come on."

I lead him to the kitchen. Unlike the last visit where he made himself at home at the kitchen table, the detective remains standing as I pour the coffee. I can feel his gaze on me.

I hand him a mug and keep one for myself.

"So," he says as he leans against the counter opposite of me. "What's going on with Ian?"

"I don't know. I haven't seen him or heard from him in two days. Considering you are all up in my personal business, I wondered if you had seen or talked to him."

Stahl ignores the jab. "Why did he leave in the first place?"

"We got in an argument."

"About what?"

"The usual."

"Money?"

"Kind of."

"Infidelity?"

"Kind of."

"Tell me about the argument."

"Well, to be honest with you, I told him that you came by the house and asked about his business and made implications that it wasn't doing so well."

"And how did he take that?"

I open my arms to reiterate that Ian is not here. *Not well, obviously.*

"Okay, and what about the infidelity part?"

I sigh. "I believe Ian's cheating on me. Has been for a while."

"So *he's* cheating on *you*—not the other way around?"

I narrow my eyes. "Listen, I talked to Jenny at the Diner about what *you* said she said. About accusing Ian and me of having an affair while I was still married to Jack. She said she didn't remember ever saying that. Want to know what I think?"

"Very much so."

"You made it all up. To get under my skin."

"Don't flatter yourself, Ms. Abbott. And I thought this meeting was about your missing fiancé, not you. So, tell me, who do you think he's running around with behind your back?"

"I'm not a hundred percent sure. But all the signs are there."

"What kind of signs?"

"The usual—Ian isn't too creative. Lots of phone hiding, working late hours, a sudden desire to run errands late at night, and last but not least, ice-cold sex."

I watch the detective over the rim as I take a sip of coffee. I don't get the reaction I was hoping for. And what was I hoping for?

"So, let me get this straight," he says. "I start digging up the past—getting 'all up in your personal business,' as you say. Then you two get into an argument, and Ian leaves and ghosts you."

"In a nutshell, yes."

"Did you tell him that I implied that Jack's death was no accident, that you guys used his insurance money to fund Ian's business?"

"Yes, he picked up on that immediately, Detective. He's not stupid."

"No, I don't think that he is. And I don't think you are either."

"What's that supposed to mean?"

"You're manipulating me."

"Am I?"

"Yes. I believe every word that comes out of your mouth has ulterior motives, and every move you make is calculated."

"So, you're saying that me calling you to discuss my concern for my missing fiancé has ulterior motives?"

"Yes. You're wanting the investigation redirected to him, *and off you.* You're wanting me to think that perhaps Ian acted alone in Jack's death—assuming there was foul play in the first place—so that he could get the money for his business."

"Detective Stahl, I called you because my fiancé is missing. That's it."

He narrows his eyes, staring at me for a minute. "Do you realize what you're doing?"

"Indulge me."

"Let's say I take the bait and that I think, 'Yes, it is suspicious that Ian skipped town right after I implied that he was involved in Jack's death,' and then I begin to put together a case against Ian. You are essentially ruining the man's life. The man you supposedly love and agreed to marry."

I flick a piece of lint from my elbow.

"You're something else, you know that, Betts?"

"I do. But Ian is still missing, and that's a fact. No matter how you spin it."

Stahl sips as he thinks for a minute. "Okay, tell me. When was the last time you saw Ian?"

"The night of the argument, the day you came over."

"Did he pack a bag?"

"Nope."

"And I'm assuming you haven't seen his car anywhere in town?"

"Nope."

"What does he drive again?"

"A tan Subaru."

"How many times have you tried to call him?"

"Countless."

"Voicemails?"

"Yes."

"Have you checked his mistress's house?"

"Yes."

"I thought you said you didn't know who she was."

"I have my suspicions."

"If you want me to find your fiancé, you need to tell me who you think he's banging."

"Carmen Marquis."

"Really?"

"Really. Does this surprise you?"

"Shouldn't it?"

I shrug.

"Do you think she's that type?" he asks.

"I think she's all sorts of types."

"What do you mean?"

I spread my palms. "Just get that vibe."

"You know her then, don't you? More than just the gossip." When I say nothing, he presses. "She comes to your clinic, doesn't she? She's a client of yours, isn't she?"

I say nothing.

He tilts his head to the side. "You're a smart woman, Betty Lou. So, why in God's name did you really think you could get away with operating a secret clinic in this small town?"

Rather than answer, I flick another piece of lint onto the floor.

"Exactly. You don't care. You don't care about breaking

the rules, just like you don't care about throwing your fiancé under the bus. As long as it suits you, you're fine with it."

"Are you here to lecture me about my shortcomings?"

Stahl crosses his arms over his chest, regarding me closely. "You intrigue me."

"Because I can drink two bottles of wine a day and still remain a fully functioning adult, or because I am mentally ill?"

"All of the above."

"Did you really think I wasn't going to find out that you've spoken to half of Arkansas about me?"

Grinning, he tilts his head to the side. "Or is it that I didn't care if you found out?"

"Ah." I grin back. "Just like I don't care about my patients finding out that my clinic is bullshit. Touché. I see what you're doing."

"Stay away from Carmen."

"Or what?"

"Stay away from Carmen."

"Tell that to her. Tell that to the black rose she leaves on my husband's grave every year just to fuck with me."

"Why do you think it's her?"

"I know it's her."

"Jack was very loved in this town. It literally could be one of hundreds of people."

"She had a black rose sitting on her passenger seat the other day. She's up to something. More than just having an affair with Ian."

A long moment of silence stretches between Stahl and me.

The detective seems to consider his next words carefully. "You'd better be careful with this trail you're blazing through Weeping Pines. You never know, you might cross someone just as fucked up as you are, Betty Lou."

"I think I already have." I look him up and down. "Did that woman found dead in the woods the other day—Edith —really hang herself, Nicholas?"

"Appears that way. Why do you ask?"

I cock a brow. "Just kind of funny that she was your childhood nanny growing up."

"And how do you know that?"

"Jack told me. When I saw the news, the name rang a bell."

Nicholas doesn't respond.

"He also told me that she abused you, along with your parents."

"Birds of a feather."

"Did you kill her, Nicholas?"

"Did you kill Jack, Betts?"

"Nope."

"Then, nope."

I cross my arms over my chest. "What are you really doing with Jack's body, Nicholas?"

"I told you—just making sure nothing nefarious happened."

"I don't understand why you think something nefarious happened in the first place."

"Just a hunch, kind of like the hunch you just hurled at me." He sets his coffee cup on the counter. "I'll see myself out."

I stand there for a minute, adjusting to the abrupt departure. Then I follow him. "Are you off to figure out what happened to my fiancé?"

"Something like that." Stahl opens the door, steps

outside, and pauses to look over his shoulder. "Lock your doors tonight, Betty Lou."

"I always do."

"And stay close. You'll hear from me very soon."

I smile. "I'd be disappointed if I didn't."

27

BETTS

Three and a half years earlier

Twenty-five grams of pure-grain strychnine for one hundred fifteen bucks—it is truly shocking what you can buy on the internet.

I hid it in a shoebox in my closet.

I didn't touch it for weeks while I meditated on my plan.

In the end, I decided to let fate decide the course that this would take. After all, who am I to dole out life or death?

So, one night, while Jack was out of town, I retrieved the poison from the box, tiptoed into the kitchen, and poured two hundred times the indicated amount into what remained of my husband's most coveted bottle of bourbon. I shook it up, watched the tiny granules dissolve, then replaced the bottle and went to bed.

Days went by, weeks. Months. Every few days, I would check the bourbon, shake it up, and put it back, until eventually I forgot about it. After all, it was in fate's hands now. If Jack decided to have a glass of bourbon, that was on him— his fault, not mine.

Just like how he decided to cheat on me. It was on him—his fault.

Not mine.

28

BETTS

Present day

*I*t's cold on the shore. The wind is biting, the waves are crashing.

My hands are stuffed in the pockets of my tweed coat, my shoulders hunched, head down.

I am barefoot, my jeans rolled to my ankles. The slip-on ballet flats I left the house in are now somewhere in the ocean, rolling on the waves. I chucked them a mere five minutes into my walk, unable to stand the sand trapped between my toes.

It is a one-mile walk from the boardwalk to Carmen's house. I've timed it perfectly, at dusk, when there is still enough light to see, but dark enough to turn on a lamp inside.

I see her silhouette in the window, her long black hair trailing behind that tall, slender body. Then I see someone else. A man.

My pulse skyrockets.

I watch them for a moment, my hair whipping in the

wind, tiny strands dragging across my eyeballs.

I am suddenly overwhelmed by a wave of sadness and despair. Of total melancholy. The anguish of realizing your life is nothing but a deep black pit of misfortune.

Tears well in my eyes. I begin to tremble.

It is hopeless.

I am hopeless.

A tear escapes and slides down my cheek, the feeling of wetness against my skin almost startling.

Is this crying?

It has been so long since I've cried.

As the silhouettes move through the little cottage, I am pulled back into time, memories blending with the present.

Three and a half years earlier

"Betts, baby, what are you doing? It's two in the morning."

I turn just as Ian steps into the kitchen, his hair mussed, his eyes swollen with sleep.

I freeze in place, hovering over the kitchen table.

Ian scans the items on the table—the crystal bottle of bourbon, the bag of rat poison, my empty wineglass. He frowns, squinting at me.

I slowly straighten, my fingers wrapping around the pair of scissors I used to open the bag of poison.

"What are you doing?" he asks again in a confused, gravelly voice.

It feels like a solid minute slides by, me staring at him, him staring at me.

As I watch, the haze sweeps away from his eyes, replaced by sudden alertness. Shock. But he says nothing.

I set the scissors onto the table. His lips part as I round the table, meeting him in the doorway.

"Betts . . . what the—"

"Shhh . . ."

I drop to my knees, pull out his penis, and slip it into my mouth.

29

BETTS

Three years earlier

It was a normal enough day.

I'd made Jack his favorite dish. A big plate of homemade chop suey over white rice. A boiling pot of stew to keep us warm during the frigid night.

We ate dinner together in silence. As usual.

After dinner, I took my bottle of wine downstairs to the basement (also, as usual), which was in the process of being renovated for a home office. I wasn't quite sure what I was going to do in this office, but I had no doubt I would find something. Bottom line, I needed a place that was mine—all mine.

It was eleven thirty at night.

I was sitting on the couch I'd had Jack drag downstairs for me, wearing a lavender nightgown as I scrolled mindlessly through social media. Specifically, an account that belonged to a woman named Carmen Marquis. A Weeping Pines native who escaped the small-town life and made a name for herself by writing smut suspense. I found myself jealous of this beautiful woman and her self-made success.

That night, I made the decision to try my hand at writing. How hard can it be?

I was deep in a daydream of becoming a bestselling author when I heard a loud thud upstairs.

I lowered the phone to my lap and frowned up at the ceiling.

Heard another thud.

At first, I thought someone had broken into the house.

I hesitated about what to do next—hide in my office, run outside, or call the police? Then I remembered my loving husband.

My heart racing, I hurried up the basement stairs.

The house was dark, save for a few dim night-lights in the corners. I was halfway to the kitchen when I heard a horrible, spine-chilling moan.

I spun around and ran to the source of the sound, the master bedroom. A sliver of yellow light from the cracked bathroom door cut through the pitch-dark room.

A shadow moved erratically behind the light, accompanied by loud wheezing and gasping sounds. Then came a desperate, gargled plea: "Betty . . ."

I lunged into the bathroom.

In nothing but his boxers, my husband was against the wall, his knees locked as he slowly slid down it. He was deathly pale, sweating, clawing at his throat and gasping for air. His eyes were fluttering wildly, his tiny pupils darting around like pinballs. He crumpled into a heap on the floor, and his entire body began to shake in wild, palsied shudders. Foam leaked from his nose and mouth.

At first, I thought he was having a heart attack.

"Jack!" I screamed and fell to my knees next to him.

For a second, his eyes were on mine, then his body stilled—no moaning, gasping, or crying. His expression went completely flat.

"Jack, *no.*"

Panic gripped me. I straddled his body, which was limp now. His eyes were open but rolled back in his head.

I began screaming, pounding his chest, performing CPR to the best of my ability.

One, two, three, breathe . . .

One, two, three, breathe . . .

But it was no use. I stopped trying to resuscitate him.

I sat there, straddling him, frozen in place. Stunned. I don't know how long I sat there. It felt like ages, but I'm sure it wasn't more than a minute.

The house was eerily quiet. I remember thinking simply:

Okay. My husband is dead.

Now what?

I pushed off of him, suddenly disgusted that my skin had been pressed up against a dead person's.

I grabbed a towel—still wet from his shower—and wiped down my legs, then washed my hands, wrists, forearms. I couldn't get the feel of him off me fast enough. It felt like ants crawling where our bodies had touched.

Once satisfied, I dried myself. His legs were in the way, so I had to step around him to rehang the towel.

Then I stepped out of the bathroom. Realizing I forgot to turn off the light, I turned, flicked the switch, then left the bedroom.

I retrieved my cell phone from the basement and called 911.

"Nine one one, what's your emergency?"

"M-my husband . . ."

"Ma'am, I need you to speak up."

"Yes—sorry. My husband . . . he's—something's happened."

"Ma'am, are you okay?"

"Yes, yes. My husband—I think he's dead. I think he had a heart attack."

"Is anyone else in the home with you right now?"

"No."

"Are you harmed in any way?"

"No."

"Okay, please give me your address."

I rattled off the address to the famed Gadleigh Estate.

"Okay, ma'am, somebody's going to be there very soon. What exactly happened to your husband?"

"I think a heart attack. I don't know. He just collapsed."

"Are you next to him now?"

"No. Hang on." I spin on my heel and hurry to the bedroom. "Yes, I am now."

"I'm going to walk you through a few things, including CPR—"

"I did. I tried that." I knelt next to Jack's body, careful not to get too close.

"You were unable to revive him?"

"Correct."

"Okay, I'm going to have you check for a pulse."

After confirming there was no pulse, the dispatcher advised me to step away from the body. I had just stepped into the bedroom when the sound of sirens broke the silence.

I disconnected the call, then flicked on the bedroom lights.

Headlights bounced off the walls, the noise deafening as the cars slid to a stop outside the front door.

And that's when I saw it.

An empty highball glass on the nightstand, next to what remained of Jack's favorite bourbon.

30

BETTS

Present day

This time, I bypass the boardwalk and park my BMW on the side of the road, finding a discreet space behind two firs.

While checking the rearview mirror, I pull on my black raincoat and slip my keys and cell phone in my pocket. Before getting out, I pull up my hood.

The rain is a deafening buzz of white noise, the wind biting cold. This is it, I think, autumn is slowly fading into winter.

My favorite season.

Head down, I pick my way through the woods, following the path I'd spent the last two hours studying on a map.

Again, I chose dusk as my timing, although tonight, it is nothing more than a blue glow filtering through dark cloud cover.

I need to be quick.

My steps are light, my stride confident as I emerge from the safety of the woods and step into the open. The shoreline is vacant of people, the sand broken up only by a sporadic clump of reeds, bent against the rain as if bowing their heads in defeat. The salty, briny smell is so strong you can taste it.

With each step, my running shoes sink deeper into the wet sand. It reminds me of one of those nightmares in which you are trying to get away from something, but your legs are too rubbery to run.

My scrutiny is pulled to the dark, churning water, then up to the angry, spitting sky. I close my eyes, feel the cold rain wet my face. Everything feels so vivid, like Mother Nature is sparing nothing on this night. The colors, the smell, the taste, the temperature, everything is turned up to the max.

I walk along the shoreline, careful to keep my pace in check. Mustn't seem too eager.

My gaze moves from one house to the next as I pass. I find myself wondering what the rich people in each home are doing. Lying, I muse. Pretending to be happy while going through the motions of a normal routine. In one form or another, at least one person in every home is guarding a secret.

Just like Carmen. Perfect on the outside, a web of lies on the inside. I know why she is so good at writing. She is fucked up, and she translates these dark, disjointed thoughts onto paper.

I have a confession.

Carmen Marquis is the entire reason I started writing. When Jack and I moved to Washington, I'd heard about the Weeping Pines native who left the small town and found fame writing. Carmen was idolized by the locals, whereas I was shunned. I figured if she could gain admiration from writing, I could too. I just needed to find my niche.

Carmen's house, the last on the cliff, is lit up. Every room is glowing with light.

I am careful to keep my hood pulled low as I study the cottage, recalling the blueprint I'd received from the previous owners, whose information I'd pulled—far too easily—from the internet. I'd called them, pretending to be Carmen, and said that I was contemplating renovations and would be delighted if they could forward me the blueprints, if they had them.

"Oh yes, yes," they'd said. "What's your email address, Carmen?"

The kitchen and living room are lit to full capacity, but her bedroom only minimally lit. Perhaps from a candle or two.

A silhouette passes by the window. Then another . . . broader.

Ian.

I pivot, then cut up the shoreline to the cliff.

The rain is falling harder now. Thunder rumbles in the distance.

I find the footpath that leads to Carmen's backyard in no time at all.

The sand is slick, challenging my ascent. The only way I can reach the top is by bending at the waist and clawing upward like an animal.

Once I reach level ground, I am breathless, my chest heaving.

But I don't stop.

Ducking down, I sprint across the yard, leaping over puddles. I slam my back against the side of the house and take a second to catch my breath. I underestimated how hard climbing the footpath was going to be.

Music comes from somewhere inside.

I am careful to avoid the windows as I pass through the shadows.

I squat behind the railing of the back patio, which runs the length of the home, and there I wait.

And wait.

And wait.

The volume of the music increases, as does the drunken laughter, from both him and her.

Finally, sometime around midnight, the living room lights click off and the couple disappear into the bedroom.

I climb over the rail and hide in the shadows outside the bedroom. A window is open, allowing me to hear movement in the room.

My heart starts to pound.

I can hear them kissing. I hear her moan. I can practically feel the pheromones pouring out of the window.

Whore.

Hatred bubbles up my throat like hot, sour bile.

The bed squeaks as they fall onto it.

My pulse is deafening, beating like a war drum as I pull the pistol from my waistband. Hands trembling, I straighten and step out of the shadows, directly in front of the sliding glass door.

They don't see me at first.

The lights are off, but as I suspected, candlelight dances along the walls.

She is naked, on all fours, groaning in delight as he rides her from behind, fisting her hair in one hand, gripping her waist with the other. Exactly as he's fucked me so many times before.

I raise the gun.

His head turns, and although his face is concealed by shadows, I know—there is no question—that our eyes meet.

Yes, my dear fiancé, I've caught you.

You cheating motherfucker.

He says something to her, then slowly pushes off the bed and turns toward me. Carmen sees me and whimpers in fear, pulling the covers around her naked body as she scrambles to the headboard.

My hand is shaking, my vision blurred from the rain pouring down my face.

He is saying something to me, slowly walking toward me, but I am transfixed on Carmen's naked outline on the bed.

Whore.

Someone yells.

I pull the trigger.

Glass explodes everywhere. Into the air, in my face, in my hair, catching like crystals in the rain.

I watch her body fly backward from the punch of the bullet, see the blood splatter against the wall.

Screams. So many screams.

I watch her convulse. I watch strings of blood spew out of her mouth. I watch her drag in her last breath as her body slumps over.

It's done.

He lunges toward me as I turn the gun on myself.

Only it's not Ian.

It's Detective Stahl.

Click.

31

BETTS

*L*et me tell you something, it is a jarring experience to wake up and you realize you aren't dead.

For a moment, I think I am sliding into the afterlife. You hear stories about seeing a bright white light, or seeing the faces of loved ones as you pass from this realm to the next.

Me? I felt like my head was about to explode. There was no white light, no flashbacks, no creepy faces, just a splitting headache accompanied by what felt like terrible motion sickness.

I squint against the light, blinking madly, trying to understand where I am.

The last thing I remember is pressing the barrel of my gun to my head and pulling the trigger. However, despite this, it appears that my head, as well as my body, is in one piece.

An ominous large figure looms over me. God? Satan?

I try to focus, but the intense concentration only makes the nausea worse. A groan escapes my lips, one that sounds disconnected from my body.

The figure slowly squats next to me, a cacophony of popping joints echoing in the silence.

"You're waking up," a masculine, gravelly voice says.

My body stills.

I know that voice.

I am dead—I must be. It is the only explanation.

I attempt to roll over but am halted by a blinding pain above my left ear. I reach up and delicately touch the spot. My fingertips come away with blood.

A spike of adrenaline rushes through my body when I realize I'm hurt. Badly. And suddenly, I am very alert.

My vision steadies as I stare up at the man, his identity slowly revealing itself to me like a puzzle clicking together piece by piece.

My pulse skyrockets as I stare up at my husband, Jack Holden. The husband whom I buried six feet in the ground, six months earlier.

The husband who should be dead.

But he is not. He is here, very alive, staring right at me.

I realize then that I am on a cold, hardwood floor in a small, dark cabin that I don't recognize. I can feel heat on the left side of my body, can hear the hissing and popping of a fireplace.

"What happened?" I croak out.

"Your gun jammed."

"Is this a dream?"

"I wish, Betts. Trust me, I wish." He stands.

I watch my husband lift a glass of whiskey from a coffee table, then settle into an evergreen armchair across from me, leaving me writhing on the floor. He crosses his legs—the way he used to when we would talk about something serious, usually money—and sips his drink, eyeing me over the rim.

"You've really fucked things up," he says.

"You're dead," I say, still trying—unsuccessfully—to wrap my head around this bizarre situation I've found myself in.

"Almost," he says. "If your fiancé didn't have a conscience, I would be dead, yes."

"W-what? Ian?"

Jack nods, then sips and swallows. "He told me about the poison—that he saw you pouring rat poison into my bourbon."

"You're a liar."

He tilts his head back with a laugh. "Well, isn't that the pot calling the kettle black?" He takes another sip. "Maybe I should clarify. I took the man you were having an affair with out for drinks under the ruse of a business discussion. Got him drunk, made him talk, slipped him a roofie, and sent him home. Kid didn't remember a damned thing."

I vaguely remember Ian becoming extremely sick in the days following him seeing me with the poison. The stomach flu, we both thought it was.

"How did you know?"

"About you and Ian? Or about the poison?"

"Both."

"Shit, Betts, a cheater can—and always will—recognize another cheater. Add that to the gossip of a small town? Everyone saw you two getting cozy behind my back."

I close my eyes. "I always hated Weeping Pines."

"I know you did. I know."

"And the poison?"

"I checked your damned receipts, Betts. God, you're stupid. Combining your affair with your sudden interest in rat poison raised a red flag. Obviously."

I close my eyes. This is all too much to process. But then

Carmen's face pops into my head. Her eyes when the bullet hit her. The blood splattering on the wall.

My face must have paled because Jack laughs again.

"Yeah, you got her," he says. "She's dead."

"Where's Detective Stahl?"

"Last I saw, trying to bring her back to life."

"Wait . . ." I attempt to sit up, my thoughts spinning.

"Don't *fucking* move," Jack barks in a tone that chills every muscle in my body.

I sink back to the floor and lie on my back like a dead body, staring up at my now very alive husband.

"Stahl saw me shoot her, right?" I ask.

"He did. And you'd be in jail right now if not for me."

"What happened?"

"I followed you to Carmen's, watched the whole damned thing. What the hell, Betts?" Jack shakes his head in a way that reminds me of a father shaming his toddler. "Anyway, in the chaos, I knocked you out with an empty flowerpot I found on the deck and dragged you away."

"So, Stahl doesn't know where I am?"

"No. Nor does the police department, which is unquestionably hunting you down, as we speak, for the murder of Carmen Marquis."

I close my eyes. Exhale.

It's too much to process.

"So, where am I?" I ask, scrubbing my hands over my face.

It is morning now, a dark, dreary day framed by the single window in the cabin. Somehow, I made it from the floor to the couch. I am wearing a long T-shirt, one of Jack's, and a pair of socks.

"A cabin," he says. "About seventy miles northwest of Weeping Pines."

"Your cabin?"

"For now, yes."

I take a second to catalogue my surroundings. I am in a small one-bedroom, one-bathroom cabin with a fireplace and a tiny kitchenette. The only furniture in the living room is a couch, a chair, a coffee table, and three—*three*—bookshelves packed with books. It is dark and cold, and it smells like earth and mold.

I draw in a jagged inhale, slowly release, then consider Jack, who is pushing around bacon in a frying pan as if everything is completely normal.

"You're going to have to explain this to me, Jack. I'm a bit ... confused."

"You're always confused, Betts."

"Let's not make this about my mental issues, okay?" God, what an old fight. One that we have had over and over—*and over*—again.

"Everything is about your mental issues, Betts. The entire world revolves around it." He glances over his shoulder.

He looks good, I realize now that I am in a clearer mental state. He's lost weight, grown out his hair, and also grown a beard, giving him a sexy silver-fox appearance. The flannel shirt he's wearing adds to the relaxed, casual vibe that I am unaccustomed to.

Jack places the bacon on a paper towel. "Once I realized you were going to try to kill me—Jesus, Betts, seriously? For cheating on you?" He sends me another disapproving glare over his shoulder before continuing. "I started making plans. Honestly, at first, I didn't know how I wanted to approach the whole thing. It isn't every day you find out your wife intends to kill you."

"I literally gave CPR to your *dead* body. I called the cops. They came and took you away in a black bag, Jack. How the hell did you do it?"

"Eddie." Jack grins as he cracks an egg into the frying pan. "The guy who runs the morgue? He and I went to high school together. Good guy. And the responding officers? Friends of his."

"You staged the entire thing?"

He points the spatula at me. "Bingo."

"You sick fuck."

"Hey, I'm not the one who killed her husband."

I roll my eyes, then look around the cabin. "So, what?

You've been staying here? Hiding out, since everyone thinks you're dead?"

"Yep." He contemplates the view out the window. "It's peaceful out here."

"Does anyone know you're here?"

"No."

"What about Eddie? His buds?"

"They think I skipped town after everything. Moved abroad." He flips the eggs with flair, just as he did when we were married. "I've gone into town twice to get food and eavesdrop on local gossip. No one recognizes me with the long hair and beard, although I wear glasses and hats just to be safe."

"What about Stahl?" I ask. "He dug up your grave."

"He dug up an empty casket."

"Jesus, Jack!"

"I know—can you imagine? Poor kid. I didn't expect that. He's a dog with a bone when he's got his mind on something."

"He thinks I killed you."

"Suspects it, yes."

"And now he dug up an empty casket."

"Which probably makes him even more suspicious of you, huh?"

"I still don't understand what he was going to do with your bones."

"Run toxicology tests on them, if I had to guess. Certain poisons, including strychnine, stay in bone marrow long after death."

I shake my head. "Smart guy."

"Not that any of that matters anymore, because everyone knows you're a murderer now, despite what you did to me.

The county detective literally saw you kill someone in cold blood."

"I thought she was fucking my fiancé."

"She wasn't."

"Yeah, I get that now."

"Rumor has it, she and Stahl have been together for a while now. You know they were high school sweethearts? Anyway, she quit writing to train to become a detective, just like Stahl."

I chew on this a minute. So, that explains Carmen's mysterious hiatus from writing.

I tilt my head to the side. "Where is my fiancé? Ian?"

"Emptied his business account and took the first flight to Aruba the night he walked out on you." Jack plates the eggs and bacon—one egg, two slices of bacon—exactly as he did when we were married. "Finally got fed up with your shit."

It doesn't surprise me. Ian was never strong enough to handle a woman like me.

I glance at the trees outside, then back to my husband. "It's you who has been watching me from the woods, isn't it?"

"Yep."

"What were you going to do? Haunt me for the rest of your life?"

He shrugs. "Figured it's the least I could do to the woman who intended to kill me." He slides a plate on the coffee table in front of me, then sinks into the armchair and balances his plate on his lap. "Eat."

I stare at the food. I'm not hungry, and even if I were, I'm willing to bet my life that it is not salt sprinkled on top of those eggs.

"You're asking all the wrong questions right now, Betts."

Jack slices into his egg, sending a wave of yellow yolk pooling on the plate.

"What should I be asking?"

"You understand you're a fugitive now, right? The entire state is hunting you in connection with the murder of Carmen Marquis. Stahl will never, *ever*, quit hunting you."

Yes, things have definitely spun out of my control.

I turn my head to Jack, who is staring at me. "Why haven't you killed me?"

"Give it time," he says with a wink. "For now, eat. Then fix your head. I've got bandages and hydrogen peroxide set out in the bathroom."

BETTS

*T*hree days. For three whole days, we go on like this.

Jack and I—him presumed to be dead, me a fugitive on the run—watching each other like hawks from opposite sides of the cabin. Both walking on eggshells while waiting for the other to strike.

Who will kill whom first?

Three days of this. It is exhausting.

Still, he hasn't made a move to kill me. And I haven't tried to kill him either.

Honestly? I think Jack doesn't know what to do with me.

I think he likes the company. Jack always was a gregarious man.

We spend the days reading—Jack has no fewer than two hundred books stored in this cabin. He always liked to read. I've read eight novels in the last seventy-two hours.

We are never out of each other's sight. Ever vigilant, ready to attack if needed.

I only eat the food I prepare. Jack does the same. He won't touch anything that I have without washing it first.

In the evenings, I pretend to sleep, angling myself on the couch so that I can see the bedroom door, waiting for him to come out and shoot me. I sneak catnaps behind the locked bathroom door while I pretend to shower.

I have nowhere to go. No car, no money, no credit cards, no change of clothes, nothing. Even if I did, I would be arrested immediately.

I am in a pickle.

Jack knows this.

Funnily enough, there is something about this game of cat and mouse that arouses me. I've never seen this side of my husband before. I've never felt this exciting spark of danger from a man.

And just like that, I decide it's time for more.

Once again.

More.

He is washing the dishes when I come up behind him, a kitchen knife clutched in one hand.

I don't touch him at first.

He senses me and stills.

The corner of my lip curls up.

A second slides by as Jack decides what to do next, and I have no doubt he is searching for the knife that was there a mere minute earlier.

I rise on tiptoe to breathe against his neck. "Want to play a game?"

"What kind of game, my dear wife?"

I press the tip of the knife against the vein pulsing in his neck.

Slowly, he turns, his eyes ablaze with emotion.

Before I can speak, he grabs my wrist and crushes his lips onto mine. His tongue swirls in my mouth as he twists my wrist, sending a sharp pain shooting through my hand.

The knife hits the floor no sooner than he pulls another from the drawer behind him.

He spins me around and pins me face-first against the refrigerator. The tip of the blade pierces my neck as he unbuttons his pants and pulls up my T-shirt. There is no underwear to wrestle off. He bends me at the waist, positioning me as he sees fit.

The breath whooshes from my lungs as he thrusts into me with so much power that my cheek slams against the refrigerator.

I lean into the tip of the knife, feeling the blood trickle down my neck as my husband takes me from behind.

A glass vase falls from the top of the fridge, shattering on the floor.

Blood leaks down my shoulder, down my arm.

"Harder," I grind out. "*Harder*."

The whole thing lasts not even two minutes.

Afterward, our chests heaving, dazed and sated, we say nothing as we split a bottle of wine.

*J*ack and I have sex seven times over the next forty-eight hours.

I don't know what time it is, what day it is.

I don't know up from down.

There is no television in the cabin, so I have no idea how the manhunt for me is going. The story could have hit national news, for all I know.

Jack and I are literally hidden in the mountains, off the grid, cut off from the world.

It is snowing. A dark, cold, quiet night.

I climb out of the bath Jack drew for me, throw on his robe, and open the bathroom door.

Candlelight illuminates the living room. On the coffee table are two plates of spaghetti and two glasses of wine.

Jack is fluffing the pillows on the couch. He smiles when he sees me.

"What's this for?" I ask, stepping into the room.

"An apology."

My brow cocks.

He smiles, gesturing to the couch. "Just sit down and don't overthink it."

I do as I'm told and wait until he does the same, sitting across from me in his armchair.

"This is quite romantic."

"This surprises you?"

"It does."

"Does it? Really? What about the time I bought you those diamond earrings and hid them in your lunch?"

I smile. I do remember that. I'd finally confided in Jack that I hated my new job as the middle school counselor. The next day, I found a pair of diamond earrings in my lunch, with a note that read: *To brighten your day.*

"I thanked you for that, didn't I?" I ask.

"You didn't."

We stare at each other for a moment, and I wonder, how did things get so fucked up between us?

"Thank you," I say.

"You're welcome."

I pick up my fork. "You're going to be arrested too, you know."

"Why's that?"

"Aiding and abetting a criminal."

He shrugs. "We'll see how it all pans out."

I stab a piece of egg. "We're going to run out of food."

"Yes, we are. I'll have to figure out something soon. I didn't plan on having a roommate."

"Ah, is that what this is?"

"What would you call it?"

I think for a moment. "I don't know."

He smiles. "Eat, Betts."

We eat in silence, peacefully enjoying the fire crackling next to us, the snow falling outside.

Jack tops off my wine.

"You said this was an apology dinner. What are you sorry for?"

He pours the remaining wine in his glass, then sets the bottle aside. "I wanted to say I'm sorry for cheating on you."

I can't hide the surprise on my face.

"I am truly sorry."

"You're just saying that because I tried to kill you afterward."

He grins. "No—well, yes, but also because I really am sorry. I should have never lied to you. I should have told you. Been man enough to do what needed to be done in the first place."

I take a deep gulp of my wine. "Thank you."

"You forgive me?"

"I do."

I lower the glass but miss the table entirely. The wine slips from my hand and splatters onto the rug.

I stare at my hand as a wave of nausea washes over me.

I suddenly feel completely disconnected from my body.

It happens so fast. The searing pain in my gut, the dizziness, the headache.

The next thing I know, I am on the floor in such severe pain that I can't see straight.

Jack is standing now, casually clearing the table as if nothing happened.

"Jack," I croak out, wondering if—by some crazy chance—he didn't notice me double over in pain.

Bile rises up my throat. I begin clawing at my neck.

I hear the plates being set in the sink. The water turns on. Jack begins to whistle a happy, haunting tune.

The front door opens.

I squint through the tears streaming down my face as a man walks into the cabin.

There are voices, a casual greeting.

I try to scream for help, but nothing comes out. The world around me is a distorted haze, my vision, hearing, touch, sound, all of it completely disconnected.

I roll onto my back as the man walks over to me.

Detective Nicholas Stahl stares down at me, a cocky shit-eating grin on his face. "She's not dead yet," he says, looking at me but addressing Jack.

Jack joins him. Both men stare down at me, watching dispassionately as I gag and spit up bloody foam.

"She's getting there," Jack says.

"You use the rat poison I got?"

"Of course."

Stahl nods, then surveys the cabin. "You're keeping up the place. Did you fix that faucet like I asked?"

"Yep. Leak in the roof too. Fixed it. You overpaid for this piece of shit."

The men laugh.

"Please," I wheeze out. "Help me. Please."

My arm slides under the couch as I am rocking back and forth like a turtle on its shell. I feel something cold and hard. My fingertips dance over the heavy object.

A gun.

"You've got everything ready?" Jack asks Stahl.

"Yep, the boat is at the dock. We'll dump her body, then come back and set the place on fire. Your plane tickets are in the glove box of my truck."

I wrap my hand around the grip of the gun, slide my finger over the trigger.

"You won't come with me?"

"No." Stahl shakes his head. "Brazil is for drunks and hookers."

"I repeat, you want to come with me?"

"No. I'm staying. I'm going to be famous after this shit goes down."

My vision is wavering. There are now four men in front of me, weaving in and out of each other like a nightmarish fun-house mirror.

I'm dying.

"She's getting close."

"Good." Jack spits on me. "Fucking bitch."

I pull the gun from below the couch, close my eyes, and pull the trigger.

Sweeping from right to left, I empty the clip, and keep pulling the trigger, the gun clicking uselessly until my arm gives out.

The cabin is silent.

I feel a warm wetness slowly seep under my heels, under my legs.

A smile touches my lips just before everything goes black.

35

BETTS

Six months later

True crime is a delicate thing to write. You have to think like the characters, become the victim, become the killer, climb into his or her mind, make a nest, and hang out there for a while.

It was uncomfortable at times, writing from their points of view, but it is what the book demanded. It is what poured out of me, albeit unexpectedly, after realizing the entanglement that had become my relationship with Ian. The book wrote itself . . . I was a mere puppet in its play.

While I am confident that I nailed Stahl's character, I can't say Carmen was *exactly* as I portrayed her in my manuscript, but it is my honest interpretation. It is what I saw when I studied her, transferred through pen to paper, so to speak.

My goal from the beginning of this journey was to make the story as accurate as possible, thinking as she did, speaking as she did. Stepping into her fancy high heels. I can only hope I did her justice.

Once the plot revealed itself to me, I revisited and studied every one of our clinic appointments—Carmen on the couch, bitching about her life, and me behind the desk, pretending to care—and took notes for my manuscript. It is then that I realized that Carmen had ulterior motives in seeing me as well. I should have known when she brought up the eye-drop murder—a bored woman poisoning her rich husband. I should have known then that she was working with Detective Stahl to bring me down for Jack's death.

But there was no way I could have known that Jack never died in the first place. Through the many—many—hours of interviews the investigators put me through, I have gathered that the night I shot Carmen, Nicholas saw Jack hiding in the shadows. From that point on, they conspired against me.

And look at how well that turned out for them.

I want it to be clear here that I intended to end my life after exposing (who I thought was) Ian and his mistress, and then killing her. Everyone knows that people become more famous—more revered—after they are dead. My book would have been studied ad nauseam by psychological professionals, who would spend hours dissecting every word written by a killer. My name would be remembered forever.

I tried to kill myself—I really did. I put the barrel to my head and pulled the trigger. I would be dead if the gun hadn't jammed.

Fate, obviously, had other plans for me. And as usual, I am more than happy to oblige.

"Betty Lou Abbott," the guard calls as he begins unlocking the jail cell. "Time for cleanup duty."

I quickly close my notebook and tuck the manuscript under the thin mattress, next to the dozen letters from literary agents who have offered to represent me—the madwoman serving three life sentences for killing Carmen Marquis, Jack Holden, and Detective Nicholas Stahl.

The Widow of Weeping Pines, I've entitled it.

As the steel door slides open, I smile.

It will be my first bestseller.

★ THE RAVEN'S WIFE ★

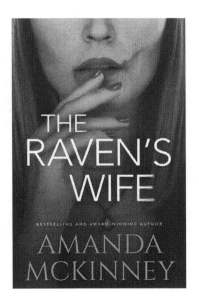

Julia Klein killed her husband. Or did she?

On a frigid winter night, Daniel Klein was stabbed to death
in his penthouse suite by his wife, Julia. At least that's what

the police report reads. The truth, however, is far more sinister.

After relocating to a remote cabin in the middle of the mountains, Julia's only goal in life is to piece together her broken past. But questions about that fateful night arise when Logan, Julia's brother-in-law, shows up on her doorstep—with evidence that things are not as they appear.

It soon becomes apparent that someone else knows the details of that night, and they will stop at nothing to ensure what happened in the dark, stays in the dark.

Julia, not unaccustomed to drama, rises to the occasion, determined never to be a victim again. After all, she has been here before.

After all, behind every crazy woman is a man who made her that way.

As the saying goes, fight fire with fire—except in this explosion, only one will survive.

COMING JANUARY 20, 2023
PRE-ORDER FOR ONLY $0.99 TODAY
(*Limited-time pre-order price*)

Sign up for my newsletter to be the first to receive details on my next release...

ABOUT THE AUTHOR

Amanda McKinney is the bestselling and multi-award-winning author of more than twenty romantic suspense and mystery novels. Her book, Rattlesnake Road, was named one of *POPSUGAR's 12 Best Romance Books,* and was featured on the *Today Show.* The fifth book in her Steele Shadows series was recently nominated for the prestigious *Daphne du Maurier Award for Excellence in Mystery/Suspense.* Amanda's books have received over fifteen literary awards and nominations.

Text **AMANDABOOKS to 66866** to sign up for Amanda's Newsletter and get the latest on new releases, promos, and freebies!

www.amandamckinneyauthor.com

If you enjoyed Widow of Weeping Pines, please write a review!

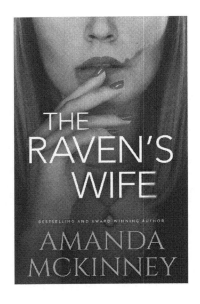

★ **MORE BY AMANDA MCKINNEY** ★

NARRATIVE OF A MAD WOMAN (THRILLER SERIES):
The Widow of Weeping Pines
The Raven's Wife (Coming January 2023)
The Lie Between Her (Summer 2023
The Keeper's Closet (Summer 2023)

ON THE EDGE SERIES:
Buried Deception
Trail of Deception (2023)

THE ROAD SERIES:
Rattlesnake Road

Redemption Road

#1 BESTSELLING STEELE SHADOWS:
Cabin 1 (Steele Shadows Security)
Cabin 2 (Steele Shadows Security)
Cabin 3 (Steele Shadows Security)
Phoenix (Steele Shadows Rising)
Jagger (Steele Shadows Investigations)
Ryder (Steele Shadows Investigations)
Her Mercenary (Steele Shadows Mercenaries)

THE AWARD-WINNING BERRY SPRINGS SERIES:
The Woods (A Berry Springs Novel)
The Lake (A Berry Springs Novel)
The Storm (A Berry Springs Novel)
The Fog (A Berry Springs Novel)
The Creek (A Berry Springs Novel)
The Shadow (A Berry Springs Novel)
The Cave (A Berry Springs Novel)

The Viper

Devil's Gold (A Black Rose Mystery, Book 1)
Hatchet Hollow (A Black Rose Mystery, Book 2)
Tomb's Tale (A Black Rose Mystery Book 3)
Evil Eye (A Black Rose Mystery Book 4)
Sinister Secrets (A Black Rose Mystery Book 5)

READING ORDER GUIDE

THRILLER BOOKS (DOMESTIC/PSYCHOLOGICAL) ↓

Narrative of a Mad Woman:
Widow of Weeping Pines
The Raven's Wife (Coming January 2023)

SMALL-TOWN ROMANTIC SUSPENSE ↓

Road Series:
Dark, emotional Romantic Suspense/Mystery. Each book is a standalone. First-person POV.
#1 Rattlesnake Road
#2 Redemption Road

On The Edge Series (NEW!):
Action-packed Romantic Suspense/Psychological Suspense.
First-person POV.
#1 Buried Deception
#2 Trail of Deception

Steele Shadows Security Series:

Action-packed Romantic Suspense with swoon-worthy military heroes and smart, sassy heroines. Must be read in order.

First-person POV.

#1 Cabin 1

#2 Cabin 2

#3 Cabin 3

#4 Phoenix (Steele Shadows Rising) - Can be read as a standalone.

Steele Shadows Investigations Series:

Action-packed Romantic Suspense/Crime Thriller. Each book is a standalone. First-person POV.

#1 Jagger

#2 Ryder

Steele Shadows Mercenaries Series:

Action-packed Protector Romance. Mystery, Exotic Locations, Swoony Heroes. Each book is a standalone. First-person POV.

#1 Her Mercenary

#2 Her Renegade

Berry Springs Series:

Romantic Suspense/Mystery. Each book is a standalone. Third-person POV.

The Woods

The Lake

The Storm

The Fog

The Creek

The Shadow

The Cave

Broken Ridge Series:

Dark, emotional Romantic Suspense. Must be read in order.
First-person POV.
#1 The Viper
#2 The Recluse

Black Rose Mysteries:

Romantic Suspense novellas. Must be read in order.
Third-person POV.
#1 Devil's Gold
#2 Hatchet Hollow
#3 Tomb's Tale
#4 Evil Eye
#5 Sinister Secrets